Janis Spehr

Ladies, a plate please

Ladies, a plate please
ISBN 978 1 76041 425 2
Copyright © Janis Spehr 2017
Cover images: vintage cup © b_lanka; vintage hatbox © Lev

'Little boxes'
Words and music by Malvina Reynolds
Copyright © 1962 Schroder Music Co. (ASCAP). Renewed 1990
Used by permission. All rights reserved

All efforts have been made to seek permission for the use of copyright material – we welcome contact from copyright holders

First published 2017 by
GINNINDERRA PRESS
PO Box 3461 Port Adelaide 5015
www.ginninderrapress.com.au

Ladies, a plate please

Also by Janis Spehr and published by Ginninderra Press
Leaving Ray
Sea Pictures

Contents

The day the ferrets went bush	7
Cinderella in the cowshit	22
Ladies, a plate please	36
Richard Tauber in a monocle	48
Tuckerbox blues	62
boy/bow-tie/flowers	73
Katherine & Phyllis	86
A white cockatoo and a pink crustacean	94
Two roses in a hatbox	109
Elizabeth attends a gay wedding in Gippsland	127

'I never wanted to fight – it was thrust on me.'
– Katherine Mansfield, 'A Swing of the Pendulum'

The day the ferrets went bush

The ferrets were dark yellow, the colour of old pee, and stunk like that too. Elizabeth peered through the wire mesh which formed a window in the wooden crate then reached for its lid.

'Hey, don't do that!' Mick yanked her hand back. 'They'll bite your finger down to the bone if you give 'em a chance.' He latched the lid then lifted Michaela into the back seat. 'You can look at 'em but don't touch, all right?' He threw his hat onto the front passenger seat, put the car into gear and drove down the road towards the general store.

Michaela had a long twig she had picked up when they stopped off at Mr Mathieson's. She kept poking the squirming, furry things, trying to stir them up. Michaela was such a baby.

Elizabeth stared out the half-open window, felt the breeze touch her neck like breath and saw the grass bowed down in the paddocks. Someone had hit a rabbit on the road and two ravens hovered overhead, accompanied by some kind of smaller bird hoping for leftovers.

They had been driving around for a while now, ever since Mum had shouted at Dad, 'Just take them! I'm sick of them! Take them away!'

'I'll take them after dinner…'

'No, take them now!'

So the three of them had got into the car and left Graeme to look after Mum and the twins. Joy had been sick again last night. Joy was always sick. Sometimes she was so sick she had to go to hospital in Town. She cried all night and then Mum shouted at them all the next day. It was worse now that Mum was in the family way.

Light flooded the grey dirt road and poured in through the windscreen.

Her father's black hair curved into white skin and one of his grey eyes winked at her in the rear-view mirror. 'This is our adventure, right, Lizzie,' he had said when they set out. 'We'll go to old Archie's and buy a couple of his critters.'

She and Michaela had sat in Mr Mathieson's small dark kitchen with the faded red lino, listening, while he and Dad had a cuppa; then they had gone outside into the shed to choose.

The car passed the Anglican church and the recreation hall.

'So, what are we going to name them, kids?'

'I'm gunna call one Shanks,' Michaela announced. Michaela called everything Shanks. Her pony was called Shanks. Michaela was such a baby.

'Shanks, eh? How about Flossie and Bozo?'

'They're stupid names,' said Elizabeth.

'Well, do you have a better idea?' Her father turned briefly and grinned.

The car swerved and hit a pothole and he swore softly as he guided them back onto the right side of the road.

Elizabeth stared down. One of the ferrets was a bit bigger than the other; the small one had darker fur, a tail that was gold with white underneath. Its gold eyes stared back as it hissed and snarled. She took Michaela's twig, and poked it, just to make it jump about, but then she forgot all about what was in the crate because as the car slowed down outside the general store, there was pretty little Julie Everett, all dressed up and coming back from a birthday party to which the Macguire girls had not been invited.

Julie wore a pink dress with a shiny satin bodice and full tulle skirt like a ballerina's. Pink gauzy fairy wings sprouted between her shoulder blades and she carried a pink wand with a shining silver star on the end. Her blonde hair was plaited and wound around her head like a crown.

'If you have a star you'll go far…' Mick sang. 'Oh, look at that girl, look at that pretty little girl! She's a real little princess!'

Elizabeth was silent for a moment then she said, very quietly, 'You only get those in books.'

'Oh, no, you find them everywhere.'

Pete Everett came out of the store, carrying a paper bag of groceries in one hand and a sack of spuds in the other. Petey liked a beer and a yarn and there was the pub, just across the road.

Mick parked and took out some of the new decimal money. 'There you are. You kids go and buy yourself an icy pole. Lizzie, you look after your sister. I won't be long.'

He always said that when he went to the pub. Sometimes he made them wait in the car or sometimes he took them inside. Elizabeth hated the smell. This was another of the things which made Mum shout. Michaela took Elizabeth's hand but Elizabeth shook her off when she saw Julie Everett watching. She didn't want Julie thinking she was a sook.

'That's a nice red jumper you've got on, Lizzie,' Mr Armitage said from behind the store counter.

'Mum got it for my birthday.'

'I haven't seen your mum for a while. Is she busy with her music?'

'No, she's in the family way,' Elizabeth said gravely and Mr Armitage laughed and called her a character.

Elizabeth bought a Choo-choo bar, musk sticks and milk chocolate buddies. When she and Michaela came out, Julie Everett was standing beside the car, looking through the window.

'What's those?'

'None of your business.' Elizabeth sucked thoughtfully on her Choo-choo bar. She didn't care about the stupid dress but she did want to hold the wand with its glittering star. 'You want to have a look?' She opened the car door and they scrambled in.

Julie Everett stared at the crate then put out her hand towards the wire mesh.

'Don't do that. They'll bite your fingers down to the bone.'

'What are you going to do with them?'

'Race them.'

'You can't do that.'

'Can so. You watch.' Elizabeth unlatched the rusty hinge on the lid.

She only meant to lift it a little but the larger ferret thrust its head through the gap and bit her finger. There was a sudden putrid rush of fur.

'Quick!'

They raced down the laneway between the store and the corrugated-iron fence of the house next door. One ferret disappeared down a drainpipe but the other made for the tangle of bracken and suckers which had grown up from piles of discarded garden waste dumped at the back of the houses lining the street.

'We'll never catch them!'

'Yes, we will!' but the ferret was an ochre streak stretched against belladonna lilies.

It reached a clutch of rabbit burrows beneath blackberry canes and vanished. Loud hideous squealing came from the burrow, then silence.

'Dad's gunna be cross,' said Michaela, panting along behind them.

Elizabeth wiped blood from her finger onto her corduroy pants. The spring rain had stopped for a few days but the track they had followed was still squelchy and her boots were caked with mud. Julie's dress was torn. Her pale pink leather slippers were sad little carcasses.

'We've gotta go back to the car…'

Elizabeth put her hands over her sister's mouth, risking another bite. There was a fence up ahead and beyond that a bank of blackberries and bracken but she saw a faint trail through it, something made by animals, silently following one another at night. She started toward the fence.

'There'll be trolls.'

'Don't be stupid.'

The barbed wire pricked Elizabeth as she crawled underneath and something tore but when she saw the orchard she forgot about the ferrets and her scratches.

'Come on.' She held up a strand of wire so Julie could scramble through.

The tallest tree waved and called from the other side of the orchard.

It was different from the others and had no fruit, just small brown polished buds, hard as stones. Elizabeth shinned up until she sat in the first and deepest cleft.

'Come on.' She held out her hand to Julie, who kept slipping and sliding; finally, she found a sure footing.

They climbed, testing their weight, yelping occasionally to each other.

'I'm going to fall!'

'No, hang on!'

'It's okay, I'm all right now.'

Small insects planed about them, irritated but not sufficiently aroused to sting. The higher they went, the smaller and lighter the branches became. Elizabeth breathed in Julie's scent of oranges and dirt.

They reached the crown, with its layer of trapped moist air and felt the sun pierce the canopy of leaves. An apple tree had thrust straggling limbs toward the oak. Elizabeth reached for some fruit, tore it off and bit, but it was just a sour old cooker. She spat it out. She poked her head through the leaves and looked down. Some of the trees were old and falling down; branches had broken off and lay around like firewood. Rotting apples were scattered on the grass and, on the other side of the fence, a bull raised his shiny muzzle.

Elizabeth pelted the bitten apple. It bounced off the big hairy rump and the bull snorted and flinched. She and Julie laughed. Julie threw an apple and Elizabeth another and they might have kept it up all afternoon except that Michaela, who was still below, whingeing and sooking, picked up an apple and rolled it along the ground.

The bull ate it! He rolled the apple around, covered it with slobber then chomped it down. He ate slowly and majestically, as though he was doing them a favour, strings of bitter green juice oozing between his jaws.

Michaela started to scramble beneath the fence towards him.

Elizabeth slithered down the tree, ripping her pants in a different place, and pulled her back. 'Don't do that. They can kill you.'

That had happened to Sharon Cartwright's uncle. His Aberdeen Angus had knelt on him until he couldn't breathe. But that was his fault: everyone said he hadn't been careful. Elizabeth gave Michaela a small push because she was such a baby, just as they heard the sound of distant shouting. Their fathers' were looking for them, telling them it was time to go home.

'Hide!' Elizabeth raced for the tree but Julie stood there, waiting quite calmly as the calling voices closed in.

She held her slippers in her hand. Her feet were soft and pink as ten little pigs. The breeze lifted her pink dress and blew back strands of her shining hair while she waited, ready to be found.

'We're here, Dad!' Michaela, that baby, raced over to him.

Both their father and Mr Everett were angry at first.

'I bet this was your idea, Lizzie.' Mick held out the empty crate. His eyes had that shiny look they got after he had been to the pub.

Julie's father said that he hadn't paid out good money for her to ruin a lovely frock; but when they saw the apples and the bull, they both started to laugh.

'Oh, look at youse, look at youse!' Mick put his free hand through the fence and rubbed the bull's ears. 'You'll give poor old Soldier the guts ache. Come on, let's go home. I'm late for the milking and your mum will be wondering where we've got to.' He took out his handkerchief and wiped Elizabeth's mouth. 'Look at you. You've been eating them black lollies again. You look like Little Black Sambo.' He swung Michaela up onto his shoulders and she clutched his hair.

Mr Everett held Julie's hand and Julie held Elizabeth's.

'He was a nice old bull, he was,' Michaela said, on the way back to the car.

Just for a moment, as Julie took the wand from the bonnet of the station wagon, Elizabeth touched the star. She felt its silveriness and wished.

Their travels had taken them in a fifty-mile circle through the district; they were not far from home.

'How about a singalong, kids?' Mick threw the empty crate in the back, the place where bags of calf feed and Scooter the dog often went.

It was Michaela's turn for the front seat so Elizabeth stretched out on the back and watched the tree tops on the side of the road flick past.

There's a track winding back from an old-fashioned shack, along the road to Gundagai…

Mick slowed down to negotiate a stretch of gravel pitted with craters.

'We always sing this song.'

'Well, it's where I was born, up in the Riverina.'

Riverina… It was a lovely word, all dreamy and green. Saying it made Elizabeth feel she was back at the top of the tree, with the light stroking her face and the smell of oranges beside her. It was strange to think of her father in some other place, a long time ago.

…where my mummy and daddy are waiting for me…

They were through the potholes and Mick drove quite fast. They skidded around corners, which made small stones fly up and hit the glass.

'Did you have a mum and dad, when you were there?'

''Course I had a mum and dad. Everyone has a mum and a dad.'

'Where are they now?'

'Gone.'

'Gone where?'

'Just gone. They're up in the sky now.'

Elizabeth sat up and scanned ahead. The tree tops disappeared; clouds and a flash of crimson rosellas filled the window.

Mick laughed. 'You can't see them.'

'Can they see us?'

''Course they can. They're always there.'

'Oh…'

'Shhh… You'll wake your sister,' but the seam of sleep Michaela had entered held until they reached the bitumen strip grudgingly laid down by the shire last year.

The road was flat as an ironed hair ribbon now and led straight back to the yellow weatherboard on the Petersens' farm.

Elizabeth thought about her mother: she might be smiling, when they got home, especially if she had been playing the piano. If she was happy she and Dad would sing, something like *Maxwelton's brae's are bonnie, where early falls the dew/ And it's there that Annie Laurie gave me her promise true...* Or perhaps it would be a faster song, *Phil the fluter's ball*, and Dad would dance, something he called an Irish jig, hopping around to make them all laugh.

But what if Mum was slamming the cupboard doors in the kitchen and shouting when you tried to talk to her? Dad would laugh, trying to cheer her up, but that usually made her shout more. Then there was no hope; they all had to wait until she was better. As long as it wasn't raining, she and Michaela went outside, into the sheds and the pony paddock.

'Feel sick...want the toilet...' Michaela said, waking.

Mick really put his foot down and they flew over the last mile. 'Well, we're not too late, kids, not too late,' he said, as they swung into the driveway with its border of blue and white agapanthus.

He scanned the paddocks, checking to see if Don Petersen was already out there because that always meant a telling off, as though he was a bloody kid at school: 'I expect better than this, Michael...'

They drove past the brick house with the dahlias and roses in the front garden and on towards the small weatherboard, where the sun coated the window panes and laid strips of light across cracked paint.

The sounds she heard, muffled but desperate, made Elizabeth look out the back window and then she started giggling. Michaela wiped the snot from her nose on her sleeve edge and joined in because Mrs Petersen looked so funny running up the driveway behind them, nearly falling over in her stiletto shoes, her bum wobbling and her bright red lipstick like a clown's. Usually she called out to them, 'Yoohoo, girls,' in a high trilling voice but today she rushed straight up to Dad's open window and spoke in a low gabbling way. Elizabeth caught a new word: convulsions. 'She was having convulsions. Don took them to the hospital, half an hour ago.'

After their father left, Elizabeth and Michaela stayed with Mrs Petersen.

'Want to go outside,' Michaela said. 'I wanna see Shanks.'

'No, no, you come along with me,' said Mrs Petersen gaily. 'Come on, Lizzie,' she said pleadingly, when she saw Elizabeth lurk reluctantly near the door. 'I don't have any little girls of my own.'

It was the first time Elizabeth had felt power over an adult, so she decided to be generous. She and Michaela followed the dress patterned with red and pink flowers into the kitchen.

'Now,' said Mrs Petersen brightly, pulling on a pair of rubber gloves. 'What shall we make?'

Later, when Mrs Petersen went into the pantry for flour, Elizabeth snuck out to see Graeme and Chris in the machinery shed but Chris Petersen shot a lacker band at her and shouted, 'Go away! You're stupid! You let the ferrets out!' He was a boy and in grade two, like Graeme.

She went inside again, cracked eggs and watched them plop into the bowl like gooey suns while she practised the new word under her breath: 'convulsions…convulsions…' She asked Mrs Petersen what it meant.

'Don't you worry about that, dear. Here, I'll help you measure out a cup of sugar.'

Michaela has been put to sleep but that was because she was a baby and only in preps. They measured and stirred then Mrs Petersen put it all in the oven, just as Mr Petersen's Falcon came up the driveway. The sun was a darker gold and in the distance the waiting cows stood in front of the dairy, bellowing because their udders were sore.

When Elizabeth raced out, her words fell over one another but as she finished, Mr Petersen laughed kindly and told her not to worry, that her mother and father had to stay at the hospital a little longer, to make sure that Joy was all right. 'So you can have tea with us, Lizzie, and tomorrow you can all go home. Now, you come inside with me because I've got to find someone to help me with the milking.'

Later, Elizabeth heard him on the phone: '…yeah, yeah, as quick as you can, mate. I appreciate it. It's just that they've got to stay in town to make the arrangements.'

Mrs Petersen had taken the cake out of the oven and it sat on the wire cooler, steam rising gently from its gold-brown crust. She mixed butter, icing sugar and a single crimson trickle of cochineal together in a bowl. She was quiet now, not silly like she usually was, spreading the pink icing with an old knife which had a dented handle. 'There you go, you poor little mite,' she said, after she had finished. 'You can have what's left in the bowl.'

They had the cake for tea, after sausages, mashed potatoes, pumpkin and green beans.

'Oh, this is a good spread, Mother, a fine spread,' Mr Petersen said, picking up the teapot and pouring.

Mrs Petersen smiled, took off her apron then sat down.

Stars had come out through the kitchen window. Elizabeth remembered Julie and the ferrets and the wand. Her father had wanted the ferrets for Graeme so that he could get money for the skins of the rabbits they caught. 'A few extra bob is always useful, even if it's only a few bob.' That's what Dad had said to Mr Mathieson. Mum and Dad were always talking about money. They talked about it then Mum went and played the piano, loudly. Now the ferrets were gone.

'Sorry,' she muttered across the table, where Graeme sat next to Chris, his chin smeared with grease.

'What's that, darling?' Mrs Mathieson put down her teacup.

'I'm sorry, sorry I let the ferrets out.'

No one said anything for a moment until Mr Mathieson picked up a knife and cut a big slice of cake. 'Don't worry about the ferrets, Lizzie. You take care of this.'

Later when Elizabeth lay in the narrow bed in the spare room, she saw the stars again. It was strange to think about a room in a house that never got used but that was because the Petersens had more money. 'They're rich and we're poor,' her mother had told her not long ago on their way home from the doctor's in Town. The Petersens' house had an inside toilet so you didn't have to worry about spiders in the dark the way you did at home; but she wanted to be home. This was Joy's fault because Joy was always sick. Elizabeth picked out the biggest star, silver like the star on the wand and made the wish again; then she heard Mr Petersen say Joy's name.

The heavy grey-painted kitchen door stood just ajar and a ray of electric light speared the patterned hallway carpet. Elizabeth stepped silently across it and listened but by now Mr and Mrs Petersen were talking about someone else.

'…and he was always a hard man, the Reverend William Cameron, thought the Battle of the Boyne was the day before yesterday.' Mr Petersen sat where he had been before, with his elbows on the table and his sleeves rolled up.

'But surely he'll contact Phyllis now. It's his *granddaughter*, for heaven's sake.' Mrs Petersen sat at the other end of the table. She had taken off her shoes and pulled on pink fluffy slippers.

'Well, he's never spoken to her since she married Mick – and he's not even much of a left-footer, never goes to Mass…'

'No, just goes to the pub…'

It wasn't right that she talked about Dad like that. Elizabeth crept back down the hallway to find Michaela in her bed.

'Scared,' Michaela said, burrowing in. 'Cold.'

'Then curl up with me.'

Mrs Petersen had taken Michaela's plaits out when she put her to bed in the afternoon and replaced them with a shiny pink plastic hair grip in front of each ear. Elizabeth slid them out, smoothed down the hair as dark as their father's, then put the stupid things in a drawer beside the bed. She placed one hand over the flannelette pyjamas and, while she wondered whether there were any beds in Town, was soothed to sleep by the distant drum of her sister's pulse.

When she woke again, it was raining and still dark. The rain was falling and falling, a big grey curtain outside the window.

'Come on.' She nudged Michaela and they tiptoed past the Petersens' bedroom, out into the yard.

The moon overhead was round and silver as a wet shilling. A single magpie let loose a ripple of notes and was answered by another. Grey light poked its way through. They held up a blanket, taken from the bed, to keep the rain off.

'Gotta see Shanks,' Michaela said, as they trudged up the drive. 'I'm gunna see him and then I'm gunna groom him.'

'Yeah, later.'

They left the blanket in a sopping heap on the washhouse floor then dashed across the concrete backyard. No one ever locked the house. In the kitchen, a few dull embers still gleamed in the stove ash. Elizabeth poked in pieces of paper but this only made smoke billow up. They started coughing.

'It stinks in here.'

Michaela went outside to where the skewbald Shetland grazed in mud. Elizabeth shut the kitchen door but the smoke followed. It was in her clothes and hair as she lay down on her bed. She could still smell it later in the morning when Graeme woke her.

'Where's Dad?' she asked, groggily.

'Milking.'

'Where's Mum?'

'In town, making arrangements.'

'Is Joy better?'

'Joy's gone.'

Elizabeth got out of bed and went to stand by the window. The sun had come out and there were millions of ants busy with the damp brown earth. She watched their scurrying and the mad tunnelling which she never understood, then looked up at the sky. It looked back, vast and silver.

On the day of the funeral, she didn't have to go to school. The whole family went to a place in Town. There was a short tree with leaves like knives out the front near the door and the light inside was brown. Michaela kept asking what was in the box sitting on the big wooden table. Mum held Gerard in her arms, rocking him, even though he wasn't making a noise.

Elizabeth had to strain around her mother's belly to see the box with the shiny handles and a bunch of white roses lying on top. They already looked floppy and some had little brown marks at the edges of their petals. A man sitting at the front played something like a piano but it made a deeper, more purring kind of sound. Her father stood holding a book open in front of him, his face a sheet of water, not making a noise either. Her mother rocked Gerard as she sang *Rock of ages/ cleft for me/ let me hide my face in thee…* These were the only sounds, the deep purr while the man played, her mother singing, steadily and strong.

Afterwards, her father carefully carried the box to a long shiny car and her parents followed it away in the station wagon. The car was black, just like Mrs Petersen's dress and hat.

'Old crow,' said Michaela, under her breath. 'Old crow, peck, peck, pecking,' but she cheered up when she saw the bottles of Marchant's lemonade and the bag of yellow banana lollies. 'Want Shanks.'

'Shhh, sweetheart. It'll soon be over. She's a little angel in heaven now.'

Graeme dug Elizabeth in the ribs. She punched him back and, in the ruckus which followed, Mrs Petersen spilt the creaming soda she had been sipping through a straw down the front of the black dress. They both sniggered as she tried to pat herself dry. A bumpy pattern showed beneath the dress, the lace from Mrs Petersen's bras. Elizabeth caught a glimpse of freckled skin and the beginnings of the dish between shallow peaks.

'Vomit,' said Michaela, quietly.

Elizabeth held her sister's hand all the way home. These were the other things she remembered later: a hot sinking burst of sunlight behind the still white face next to hers as the paddocks went by and Mr Mathieson's black and grey dog skittering out at them, hackles up and barking, trying to bite the tyres, the way it always did.

Her parents came back in the station wagon as the cows walked in single file towards the dairy, yelled at by Mr Petersen. Her father put on his work pants and old jumper and went out to do the milking. Her mother left on the dark blue dress she had worn in town, cut the stems of the two white roses she carried and filled an empty Vegemite jar from the kitchen tap. She moved around quietly, not clashing things, dropping long curls of potato peel into the sink then adding the green boats of pea pods. Michaela had been put to bed after being sick in the Petersens' car. Graeme was in the lounge room watching *Bonanza*.

Elizabeth approached the Vegemite jar carefully and sniffed the flowers. Water had made their petals curl out again but they had a funny smell, like a pile of old leaves after rain had fallen on them. Elizabeth stood breathing the smell in, as though by doing so she would draw it inside and make it disappear.

Her mother glanced across as she put the chops on the stove in a frying pan. 'Leave those, please, Lizzie.'

All through tea, the roses stood on the shelf outside the pantry and breathed their smell over the table. Elizabeth helped her mother clear the dishes, wash, dry and put them away then watched her go into her bedroom and come out carrying a round brown suitcase. She placed it on the table and unlocked it. In front of her she arranged scissors, tape and a pad of paper with thick cream pages. She separated the roses from their stems with the scissors then placed each flower between sheets of paper. Her hand clamped down gently over one rose and held it there. Small blots of damp showed through the paper. The wet leaf smell oozed and filled the room.

After she had pressed out their juice, Phyllis took the roses and placed them between clean sheets of paper then secured these between the pages of a heavy book. She lifted the book and set it down in the round box. The television had been turned off; there was not even a tap dripping or a cow calling to its calf. It was quiet.

This was what Elizabeth had wished for, that Joy would be quiet, but suddenly it seemed that, once the box was closed, the silence would go on and on.

'No!' She flung herself at her mother. She buried her head between Phyllis's breasts and felt the top of the hard sloping flesh. 'No! No, no, no!'

Phyllis calmly clamped her daughter's arms to her sides. 'Michael,' she called to her husband, who was on the back porch, rolling a smoke.

'You come along with me. Your mother's tired.' Mick lifted Elizabeth bodily, as she struggled, and carried her outside.

Elizabeth kept screaming, long past the time she knew the sound was merely theatrical. When she was worn out, her father let her go.

He lit his cigarette and leaned against the porch railing, watching a flight of birds against the sunset. 'Look, Lizzie, Cape Barren geese. They've been away nesting on the islands and now they're coming back for spring.'

Elizabeth said nothing, just stood listening until there were no more sounds from the kitchen. She thought about the ferrets and wondered where they were; would they be all right, loose in the wild? She wanted to ask her father but he seemed as far away as the birds which had passed from sight. They stood silently side by side as night fell. Released from the burden of the sky, Elizabeth quietly breathed in the smell of tobacco and the sharp oily tang of the lemon tree in the garden.

Soon all she could see was her father's cigarette and when that became a twitching red ember beneath his heel his hand rasped her neck: 'You run along, now. You've got school tomorrow.'

Cinderella in the cowshit

'Your mother's mental. Your brother's mental, too.'

'He's not a retard or anything.' Elizabeth ground out her Marlborough Red against 'Peter 4 Mandy', scratched into the pale green paint. She and Julie Everett had declared a temporary truce and were crouched down in the dunnies, occasionally beating at blue curls of smoke which floated over the cubicle wall.

'Well, he looks like a real spaz.'

Elizabeth was regretting giving away her spare surfboard, although Julie had actually asked for a tampon and then for a smoke. She almost agreed about Gerard but this made her feel disloyal to her father because it had been Mick's idea to send Gerard to the nuns, 'to see if they can straighten him out.'

'The doctor says he'll grow out of it.'

There was a faint hiss as Julie dropped her butt into the toilet bowl. 'What, when he's fifty-four?'

Elizabeth imagined leaning across, grasping the blonde hair by the roots then yanking it out. (This happened sometimes, between girls: a dispute over a boy or an item of make-up thought stolen acted like a spark on dry grass; a line of flame gusted into a conflagration with half the school as shouting audience. They were tremendous fights, the participants circling, scratching at each other then rolling over and over, their faces scarlet and scalded with tears until teachers pulled then apart.)

But then the bell went, telling her it was the end of the science period and the beginning of English.

She threw back the door, just in time to see Judith Powell, that soft shit, that teachers' pet, her hair caught in bunches over her ears, coming into the toilet early. She wanted to change her surfboard then throw it into the sanitary burner without being seen. She didn't look at Elizabeth or Julie, the stuck-up bitch, and when she entered the cubicle with the faulty lock, Elizabeth, swift as lightning, tore it out of the door and flung it against the sanitary burner. She and Julie shook with silent laughter for a moment then left Miss Goody Two Shoes stranded in the cubicle.

Outside, heat rose from the asphalt quadrangle. Their fawn cotton summer dresses, vertically striped with dark blue then gridded with grey, stuck to their backs.

Julie had recently rinsed her hair with Magic Silver White; purple streaks and patches riddled the blonde. She held an LP, the cover of which showed baby-faced Suzie Quatro clad in a leather jumpsuit, lounging with her bass guitar. 'I read in *Go Set* that she plays the electric cello. She says it gives her a good feeling between the legs.'

Elizabeth tore the wrapping off a peppermint Aero bar and proffered it. Around them the grey cinder blocks of the school rose, leaden as headstones. Sharon Cartwright, the hem of her dress riding just below her bum, waved to them but they ignored her.

'What a slack moll.' Elizabeth threw the wrapper on the ground.

'She's a real slack arse,' Julie agreed tranquilly.

The school was separated from the town by a large park of low shrubs and tussocky grass. It was common knowledge that Sharon had recently lost her virginity there with a boy from Marist Brothers. It didn't seem to have changed her, Elizabeth thought, removing her books from her locker and chewing some PK to get rid of the smoke from her breath. If anything, it had made her bossier and more sure of herself. She certainly didn't act as though she had done anything wrong.

Elizabeth pasted the gum and she and Julie moved singly, reflected like phantoms in the windows lining the corridor, towards the classroom and their different tribes. Miss Foster, the only teacher in the school who wore jeans, fumbled with the keys, then said something under her breath as kids avalanched into the room. The smell of sweat and

Impulse body spray hovered in the air. Boys festered in corners, smaller and more infantile than girls, who were completely uninterested in them, who set their sights on Form Four or Five when they wanted a date for the school social.

'…Lenane, Macguire, Mountjoy…' When she called the roll, Miss Foster only used their surnames.

Elizabeth yawned and put her head down on the desk. She had more time to sleep, now that her mother was out of hospital, but it eluded her at home. She had extra work: she and Graeme took it in turn to help Mick with the milking while Phyllis recovered. (Michaela hated the cows and her aggression towards them – sometimes she would twist their tails and hit them – always make them shit in the bail.) There was Bernie to be got off to school, although Elizabeth normally did that anyway, made sure he had a proper breakfast and had brushed his teeth before he set off on the old bike with the red mudguards. The front wheel wobbled but her brother sat up and looked straight ahead to the end of the journey, a mile and a half away.

'If you could just spare us one moment of your time, Elizabeth – boys, be quiet! The theme for today's writing exercise is Magic, so go on, get writing…'

Elizabeth yawned again and scrabbled in her pencil case. She hated these writing exercises. It was easier to read something then answer the questions about it. The red biro was closest at hand. She started, crossed out, started, changed her idea then started.

Cinderella in the cowshit

Once there lived a humble peasant girl in a small house covered in flaking paint. She lived in the house with her family and from morning to night she was put to work in the fields tending cows. The peasant girl had no proper clothes, she dressed only in rags and she didn't wear any shoes. When her feet got cold, she put them in the cow shit to warm them, which was effective but rather messy and smelly. The peasant girl had a sister who was a bitch and this bitch got all the praise because she was a good liar.

Anyway, it came to pass that the royal family who ruled the land decided to give a grand ball for their daughter's coming of age. The princess was their only daughter, a very kind and beautiful girl with waist length golden hair and an alabaster skin...

Elizabeth put the biro through *skin* and replaced it with *complexion*.

The royal family let it be known that they were keen for their daughter to find a husband and that the ball was to be the occasion for this, as well as celebrating her birthday.

Oh, how the humble peasant girl wished she could go! But the ball was only for people of noble birth and anyway, who would she go with? There was only her elder brother, ugly and hairy as a wombat.

On the evening of the ball, the peasant girl was returning home with her cows when she saw an old woman coming her way.

'You're going to find this hard to believe,' the old woman said, 'but I'm your fairy godmother.'

'Oh, pull the other one,' the girl said, but as she spoke the old woman touched one of the cows with her wand and, lo and behold, it became a low slung red sports car.

She touched the peasant girl's rags and they were transformed into a handsome dark suit. Her bare feet were shod with boots of the finest leather and her unkempt dirty hair was smoothed into a sleek pageboy.

'Now you can go to the ball,' the old woman said and vanished in a puff of dust.

The peasant girl drove to the palace, which glittered and shone with the chandeliers and the beautiful dresses of all the ladies present. The peasant girl, disguised in her boy suit, danced with them all, in their dresses of hot pink, emerald green, peacock blue and bright yellow. On a stage at one end of the ballroom, the princess in whose honour the ball was being given, clad in magnificent cloth of gold, sat between her parents.

'Pray tell me, who is that handsome boy who dances so well? she inquired and when no one could answer her question, the princess became consumed with curiosity. Boldly, ignoring her father's command to behave in a dignified and ladylike way, she descended the steps of the dais on which

she was enthroned and summoned the young man to her. 'Dance with me,' she commanded, and the two of them danced together for the rest of the evening…

Elizabeth didn't get any further than this, and anyway she thought it was fairly stupid, so she folded up one of the pages, made a paper plane and threw it at Julie.

'Oh, for pity's sake, Elizabeth…' Miss Foster held out her hand for the plane then smoothed it out. In these situations, Elizabeth was usually sent to the principal's office and sat out the rest of the period reading but today she was told to get on with her work. Instead she took the biro and wrote on the underside of the table, trying to keep the letters as neat as possible: *Sharon Cartwright is a slut and a moll.* She counted under her breath as she did this, all the way to seventy-four.

'Elizabeth, you stay behind,' Miss Foster said at the end of the lesson. While she cleaned the blackboard, she kept Elizabeth standing then pulled out a chair and sat. 'Go on.' Miss Foster indicated another chair.

Elizabeth sat, then stared straight ahead, keeping her face blank. Miss Foster was a new teacher, from Melbourne. Every second Friday, you saw her orange Datsun turn out of the car park in the direction of the highway. In the classroom discussion on War, she had mentioned she had gone on one of the moratoriums. Mick thought she was probably a communist. When she wanted to make a point she thought important, she tapped on the table repeatedly with a pencil. She wasn't pretty; she wasn't even attractive, which was probably why she didn't have a boyfriend. During a recent morning recess discussion in the toilets, Sharon Cartwright had described her as a dog.

Miss Foster handed Elizabeth the crumpled piece of paper. From outside came the disembodied shouts and screams of kids released back into the world. Elizabeth concentrated on not meeting the teacher's eyes; she fixed her own on the small beauty mark just below Miss Foster's right ear lobe.

'I know things have been difficult for you lately, Elizabeth, but you are a girl of well above average intelligence...'

'I have to catch my bus.' Elizabeth reached for her school bag.

'Just hear me out...' and then she went into the usual stuff, about how someone only had one life and how it shouldn't be wasted, blah, blah, blah...

It was humiliating to feel that you were attracting all this attention just because your mother had let down the whole family. While Miss Foster droned on, Elizabeth counted to seventy-four in her mind; she had the same number written down inside a manilla folder in her school bag, just in case she forgot.

'...so here endeth the lesson, Elizabeth, and I'm looking forward to seeing what you can do during the rest of the year.'

Elizabeth sat, her feet planted mulishly, in the stuffy classroom smelling of chalk dust and boredom. She felt she had a chance to say something but she didn't know what it was. 'Sharon Cartwright...!' she burst out.

'Sharon will never be any more then she is now, Elizabeth. Go on, go and catch your bus.'

Elizabeth successfully blocked this conversation while she waited on the narrow strip of concrete in front of the school, where the buses roiled and fumed, although she did roll 'well above average intelligence' around like a brightly coloured marble, once or twice. When her own bus finally arrived, Sharon Cartwright shoved to the front of the group of kids waiting to board then charged down the back, parking her arse on the space reserved by her friends.

Elizabeth chose a seat midway down, away from the noise and worst bullies. She neither joined in nor was picked on; this latter had something to do with Graeme, already on board because kids from the tech school were collected first. Judith Powell was stupid enough to sit in front of Graeme and Jeff Bennett so she had to endure having her hair pulled all the way to her stop. Elizabeth didn't acknowledge her brother: a lot of kids thought you were a bit soft if you showed family feeling. Across the aisle, Michaela sat with her nose stuck in *Silver Brumby Kingdom*.

Elizabeth was reading 'Her First Ball' from Katherine Mansfield's *Collected Stories*. As the bus trundled along, curving slowly around the corners on gravel back roads then rumbling over the old bridge above the Deep Creek, she glided across the dance floor with Leila. There were lights, flowers, dresses, which all became one beautiful flying wheel of lights, flowers, dresses…

'Come on, dickhead, it's time to get off.' Graeme shook her awake.

His school bag was a sad vinyl sac which held a comb and packet of Winfield. This would be his last year so he didn't bother with homework. He and Chris Petersen, who spent all his time down the back of the bus with the rowdiest girls, walked slowly ahead, school bags slung over their shoulders and ties stuffed into their pockets, discussing cricket. Early autumn light filtered through the branches of trees lining the long driveway, carrying the freshness which heralded cooler nights and the slow descent into winter.

'Come on, Dreamer,' Michaela called but Gerard dawdled behind as usual.

He had been kept back a year, had had to repeat, which was why he wore the uniform of Sacred Heart Primary. As they neared the Petersens' house, they saw Chris's mother in her garden, pruning roses. Here we bloody go, Elizabeth thought.

Mrs Petersen put down her secateurs. 'How are you, girls?' She never addressed Graeme directly; he was already outside the orbit of her motherly succour.

'Yeah, we're good, thanks, Mrs Petersen.'

'And how's your mother? I walked up to see her yesterday but she must have been asleep. Perhaps she would like some of these.' She thrust the roses at Elizabeth.

The three eldest Macguires all knew that Phyllis never answered the door to Ann Petersen, if she could avoid it. When Mick was out, she stayed at the back of the house until Ann walked back down the driveway.

'Thanks,' said Elizabeth. 'She'll love those.'

They trudged on in silence. The compassion of Ann Petersen over the recent weeks had been an awful thing to bear. As soon as she was out of earshot, they went to town.

'My husband's family were originally landowners in Norway, you know,' intoned Michaela.

'They're Chinese, they're Tasmanian…'

'…they're Hindoos,' yelped Elizabeth, chucking the cloying flowers over the fence into a tangle of blackberries.

The three of them brayed like banshees all the way to the small weatherboard house at the end of the drive. They made so much noise that Mick, standing on the veranda finishing a smoke, heard them before he saw them come around the bend.

'Look at ya!' he roared. 'Ratbags! Cranky as two-bob watches!'

Then Elizabeth knew it was all right today. Relief made her giddy; she threw Katherine Mansfield into the air, caught her then dashed up onto the veranda. 'I'm a highly intelligent girl!' she crowed. 'A highly intelligent girl!'

'Yeah? Well, you'd never know it.' Mick collected his packet of Champion Ruby and followed them inside.

Phyllis sat at the table holding the teapot, sliding it backwards and forwards over the green laminex. She looked up at Elizabeth and smiled.

'Here, I'll do that. You cut the cake.' Elizabeth took the fat pink pot embossed with gold roses and poured.

Steam lifted, fine as gauze, and hovered while Graeme and Michaela disappeared to change their clothes.

'This is good, Dad.'

'It's not a bad spread, even if I do say so myself.' Mick reached for a piece of fruit cake.

They had all taken over some of the housework: they didn't usually get fruit cake so he must have included it on the shopping list as a treat. There were some chocolate biscuits and also lamingtons Elizabeth recognised as being those Ann Petersen had left three days ago. She took a piece of fruit cake. She held the number seventy-four in her mind.

'How was school?' Phyllis carefully split a lamington in two and left it in a gaping, yellow-toothed smile on her plate.

'It was all right. Mum, did you know that Julie Everett's dad ran in the Stawell Gift one year?'

'Really? Isn't that interesting?' Phyllis, her eyes slightly unfocused, ran her fingers through Gerard's hair, bleached almost gold by the departed summer sun, as he came to stand beside her. She passed him a chocolate biscuit.

'Yeah, and Julie says that you actually have to run uphill but that wouldn't be right, would it?'

'I wouldn't know. I'm not very knowledgeable about athletics.' Phyllis held Gerard to her. Her gaze drifted across the table.

'Julie's dad came fifth...' Elizabeth was going to go on but she saw Michaela smirking, in her dangerous way, so subsided.

'Well, Petey stills looks as though he could muster a fair turn of speed.' Mick turned to Graeme, who had just come in. 'Now after the milking's finished, I want you to put the cows in the top paddock...

Elizabeth tried to think of something to say to her mother but Phyllis just sat quietly, one hand stroking Gerard's sleeve.

Through the window, a gale of cockatoos lifted from the paddock and the cows, patched, brindled and Jersey-gold, stood waiting to be robbed of their milk.

Elizabeth felt a dull obscure rage: it was a terrible thing, to be taken advantage of, year after year, and to end your days carted to the abattoir in a creaking, shit-slippery truck. 'Bloody awful,' she muttered.

'You watch your language, madam.' Mick looked at the clock on the mantelpiece and stood up. 'And help your mother with the arvo tea things.'

'Actually, I might go to the dairy this evening. Daisy and Bridie will be missing me.'

'Well....' Mick put his cup down. The doctor had stressed that Phyllis should not be overtaxed; yet it was important for her to be occupied so that she didn't have time to brood. 'Me and Graeme can manage.'

'Daisy and Bridie will be missing me.' It was true. Phyllis was best at handling the most nervous, highly strung cows, could get them to calm in a way no one else could.

As soon as they left the house, Elizabeth went straight into the bathroom, took the glass bottle from the cabinet and counted out the capsules: seventy-two. That was all right: Phyllis was only meant to take two every day. Elizabeth scooped up the remaining pills and shut the cabinet door. She changed out of her school uniform and knocked on the door of the boys' room.

'It's me, Bub.'

He was sitting on the floor with a box of brilliantly-coloured pastels and some sheets of paper. The pastels had been a Christmas present from Graeme, bought with money saved from his hay-carting jobs. Ultramarine; vermilion, rose madder: the names were like poems.

Elizabeth crouched down. 'What have you got there?'

'Sshhh.' He bent over the sheet, frowning, shielding it from her.

It was no use wheedling for a look, he would only show it to her when it was finished.

'How was school?'

'It was all right. We did art the last two lessons. How was yours?'

'Ratshit, what do you think?'

They laughed and Elizabeth left him to it, walked past the closed piano and spread her homework out on the kitchen table. Michaela was outside, lunge whip in hand, schooling the black galloway cob Chris had outgrown and that the Petersens had passed on to her as a gymkhana pony. She had stopped eating afternoon tea, said that she didn't want to get fat, and now spent all her spare time with Sparks. Elizabeth sighed and opened her geography textbook. How restful it must be to like animals; how difficult it was when you were only interested in people.

Half an hour later, she closed the book and wandered into her parents' room. She opened the wardrobe door and flicked through the rack of clothes. There was Mick's navy blue double-breasted suit with half a dozen ties slung around the hanger. Her mother's dark print dresses were neatly arranged alongside some blouses and skirts. Elizabeth opened a drawer and rummaged around among underwear and hankies. She had just refolded the boned, flesh-coloured corset with its long line of hooks and eyes which her mother put on to go into town, when she saw the hatbox down in the corner next to a jumble of shoes. Elizabeth lifted it out, sat it on the bed and tried to slide back the metal catches but they didn't yield.

She lay on the bed, contemplating chisels and knives and wondering how to describe the colour of Miss Foster's hair, when her mother came in, wearing a pair of full-waisted white cotton briefs and a cardigan over an old shirt. Phyllis never wore her dairy clothes into the house, always left them in the washhouse. Elizabeth sat up, heart jumping, preparing some ludicrous lie, but Phyllis just pulled on a skirt and low-heeled shoes then sat on the edge of the bed and stroked the brown leather lid.

'I bought this in 1951.'

'You must have been young then.'

Phyllis laughed. 'Actually I wasn't the one who bought it. My best friend and I were out one afternoon and spied this in a funny old shop. I didn't have enough money so she paid instead.'

'Was she studying the piano?'

'No, she was training to be a singer. She wanted to sing in an opera company.'

Opera: velvet curtains, screeching worse than cockatoos and love scenes which always ended in tragic death.

Elizabeth asked the question which the girls who got into fights at school would have asked: 'Was she pretty?'

'Beautiful. She had very dark hair and the misty blue eyes people from Irish families sometimes have.' Phyllis gazed past Elizabeth, smiling. 'We went to all the shows in Melbourne. We used to go out to restaurants. Oh, we had a marvellous time…'

'So what happened?'

'Well, my mother died and I had to go home to take care of Daddy and my two brothers.'

'Couldn't he have got someone else, a housekeeper or something?'

Phyllis laughed again. 'Ministers don't get paid much. There wasn't money for something like that, and anyway, Daddy couldn't have managed without me.' She stroked the lid of the hatbox but didn't open it.

'Were you really good? Good at the piano?'

'I wasn't bad, but not good enough, for what I wanted to do.' Phyllis returned the hatbox to its place in the cupboard. 'Enough of this. I've got to get the tea on. Chops tonight and I need you to set the table.' She closed the door, picked up one of Mick's shirts dropped on the floor and hung it over the back of a chair.

Elizabeth swung her legs reluctantly off the bed, thinking of the highway ten miles away which led to Melbourne. She had only been there once, on a school excursion. It took hours to reach: hours and hours.

'Mum?'

'Yes?' Phyllis half-turned in the doorway.

'What happened to your friend?'

'She became a music teacher and worked in a girls' school for a while. Then she got married and went to live in Sydney.' Phyllis went into the kitchen and took out a tablecloth. She picked up the volume of Katherine Mansfield, looked at the cover for a moment then put it down.

After tea, Mick carried in wood and lit the fire. The lounge room bulged at the seams with Macguires. There were carpet off-cuts put down over the lino; they slid around erratically and were sometimes chewed by the sofa castors. Mick and Graeme occupied either end of the sofa while they watched the ABC news. There were shots from the Asian war zone and the dark-jowled president of the United States again protested his innocence. Elizabeth curled in a chair, reading *Je ne parle pas francais*, enjoying the character of Raoul Duquette.

After eight-thirty, the television went off – Phyllis had strict ideas about that – and Bernie was shooed to bed. Gerard followed half an hour later, his mother's hand on his shoulder as she murmured about needing rest.

Mick, Graeme and Michaela played cards, Michaela overseeing the cribbage board as she sprawled before the fire. 'Two, four, six, eight and a pair of hearts is ten.'

Elizabeth was long banned from cards; the games bored her and she invariably became disruptive.

Periodically, Mick rose and replenished the fire: there was a fandango of sparks when a raw log hit the flames and a sudden hiss when they found a buried vein of sap. Burl Ives, then Peter Dawson, sang from the cabinet stereo, bought second-hand at a clearing sale. Mick had a new record featuring Father Sydney McEwan, the Irish priest. They sat listening to 'Galway Bay' and 'Star of the County Down'.

Michaela, who had recently pinned a poster of David Essex to her bedroom wall, next to all the horses, made a rude farting sound. 'This is old fogies' music.'

'Oh, you kids, you don't know anything.' Mick leaned back in the armchair and closed his eyes. The big hands, with their usual cuts and scratches healing, lay in his lap. 'Ah, listen to that, that's beautiful.'

It was so rare that Elizabeth saw her father both still and silent that she put the book down. He had found Phyllis after coming home from a day at the sale yards, bundled her up then waited for hours at the hospital while the doctors cleaned her out. He had forgotten to phone his children so that they came off the school bus to a silent house. (Bernie had been sitting in the boys' room, eating a cheese sandwich and reading a *Phantom* comic.)

'I'm afraid your mother's taken a bit of a turn,' Ann Petersen told them that evening. When she said that, Elizabeth knew immediately that Phyllis hadn't been struck down with appendicitis or fractured a limb. She knew straight away what had happened. Now, looking across at Mick, she glimpsed the daytime residue of her own nightmares, filled with limp dishevelled dolls and bloodied animals. But she said nothing, just let him sit there, enjoying the music.

A little later, she brushed her teeth, counted the capsules again then polished the bottle with the edge of her T-shirt before closing the cabinet door. On her pillow lay a leaf of paper, a pastel drawing in black and white. It was a window, without a view, an impasto space masking shadow. Something moved behind that opaque curtain, not hideous; but burdensome. Elizabeth picked it up and sniffed; it stunk of the non-smudging stuff artists used. She covered it up with some clothes, telling herself she would look at it properly tomorrow.

She woke several hours later because she needed the dunny. Michaela lay snoring, blankets twisted, no doubt dreaming about competing with the Australian flag on her saddlecloth. Elizabeth felt her usual, green-edged stab: Mich knew what she wanted.

The moon had risen and threw icy, four-paned light across the floorboards. She avoided the one which always creaked and moved silently towards the back door. As she passed the boys' room, a sound came from the lounge and she braced herself to find Gerard looming catatonically in front of the fire's embers. Sometimes he walked in his sleep and had to be guided back to bed by the family member who found him.

Elizabeth paused at the door of the lounge room. Her mother sat at the piano, playing. No, not playing: she moved her fingers across the keys but didn't press them down. There was some open sheet music in front of her which carried the composer's name: Ravel. Her mother was not-playing *Pavanne for a Dead Princess*. Phyllis didn't turn her head; the dark wells of her eyes held the moon's silver. Elizabeth wanted to run but she stood transfixed, impaled by the knowledge of what it meant to feel pain and live.

Her mother's hands formed the final chords. Without looking round she said, 'You can leave this, Lizzie. You can get away.'

Ladies, a plate please

This was the night of Josie Irving's kitchen tea.

Elizabeth picked her way through the slurry of mud and chook shit in the front yard, bunching the hem of her dress above her gumboots. She carried the high-heeled black sandals in a plastic bag. In her other hand, she held a plate of Anzac biscuits secured by Gladwrap. Graeme waited for her in the new Kingswood ute: Mick, Phyllis, Michaela and Bernie had gone ahead in the station wagon, where Elizabeth had planted *Orlando* as protection against getting bored at the dance. Above her, blue cloud smeared a lemon moon.

'Half full or half empty?'

Her brother looked up and grunted. 'She's getting fatter, I reckon.' He drove with one hand on the wheel, the other holding a half bottle of Johnny Walker which he occasionally passed to Elizabeth.

The spring air was chilly and carried a hint of rain. Lines of silver water marked the paddocks and the road was edged with starbursts of white and pink blossom. Ten kilometres from the hall, a car passed them, too close, horn blaring.

'Bloody Chris, bloody idiot,' said Graeme as the tail lights fishtailed into darkness. 'Doesn't know what he's got. If he's not careful, he'll piss it all away. Then I'll have it.'

'So how are you going to get it?'

He looked at her as though she was soft in the head. 'Work.'

That was what he had been doing for the last three years, out in the world of men. He and Elizabeth still lived in the same house but the only time she saw him now was in the evenings, briefly. Even then, he spoke mainly to Mick and Phyllis. His gaze rarely fixed on his siblings.

Elizabeth envied his solidity, his lack of deviation in purpose. She had no plans and she knew that time was running out. The exams started at the end of next month and before that there were choices to be made. All she knew was she didn't want to go to teachers' college.

The moon unfurled her sail and gilded the L-plates lying on the floor. It gleamed spectrally on the corrugated-iron roof of old Archie Mathiesons' place and the sign fixed to the gate: 'Repent! for the Last Days are Upon us!' Further along was the laneway Elizabeth had driven down a few days ago.

She pointed it out as they sped past. 'Do you know where that goes?'

Graeme glanced out; saw only darkness and the gap in the fence line. 'No, why the hell would I know?'

'I thought you knew everything.'

'I only know what's worth knowing.'

Theirs was a combat which stretched back to childhood; their silence during the remainder of the journey was companionable. They had excused themselves from leaving with the rest of the family, using the respective pretexts of ploughing and homework: now all they had to do was grab a feed, then suffer through the last set of dances and the presentation speeches. They each wanted different things from the evening. Graeme was hoping to get Sharon Cartwright to go out the back with him. Elizabeth had her thoughts fixed on the promise extracted from last night's clandestine conversation.

When they reached the community hall, festooned with balloons and crepe paper streamers, she changed her shoes. Graeme parked out the front near the road, ready for a quick getaway, where the ground was quite dry so there was no reason for her to pick up the skirt of the red taffeta dress with the ruffled sweetheart neckline as she plodded to the gate. She just hated the way the fabric stuck to the beige nylon slip, creating tiny bursts of electricity, and hated how the slip clung to the pantyhose beneath. Graeme disappeared into darkness. (There was no alcohol allowed in or around the hall but everyone turned a blind eye to the young blokes' drinking.)

Val Markham stood at the admissions door, taking money and wielding the stamp that designated 'paid'. Elizabeth held out the back of her hand for the splodgy purple elephant then crossed the hall where a portrait of the young Queen sashed with diamonds, and the honour roll bearing the names of district servicemen, decorated the walls. As she pushed open the supper room door, she saw Michaela near the stage, saucy in a scarlet halter top above a black satin skirt, an ensemble Mick had referred to as 'a Chinese hooer's outfit'.

Inside the supper room, women unloaded trays of sandwiches and sliced cakes. There was Elsie Armitage's famous ginger sponge and Doreen Wilson's rainbow cake, stippled brown, pink and yellow. There was fruit cake, jam tarts, Swiss roll, drop scones, date scones and small cakes iced with passionfruit. Tall silver urns, holding water for tea, breathed steam.

The sight of all that cake made Elizabeth feel sick. She put the Anzacs down and picked up the plate of hedgehog Michaela had made yesterday. This was Mich's speciality because it required minimal ingredients – Marie biscuits, sultanas, chocolate icing – and no cooking.

'You're a hopeless pair,' Mick had told them, leaning against the kitchen door, watching his daughters struggling with basins and trays. He picked up a tea towel and wiped a smear of golden syrup from Elizabeth's face. 'You're meant to put it in the bowl, not wear it.'

'Well, if you want something fancier, make it yourself,' but it was unthinkable that Mick do anything in the kitchen except put the kettle on. 'Ladies, a plate please', the line appended beneath all advertisements for kitchen teas, primary school Christmas concerts and fund-raising dances, meant what it said. Failure to put something homemade on the table marked a woman: a plate of shop bought biscuits said 'lazy', 'incompetent', 'sluttish'. Phyllis never even bothered with anything but allowances were made for her because of her musical contribution.

Elizabeth's hand strayed towards a piece of hedgehog, just as Elsie Armitage came bustling up.

'Now, you leave that alone, Lizzie. You can have a piece after you've passed this around.'

It was the duty of the young unmarried women to walk the perimeter of the hall, offering the contents of the plate she carried to the seated men and boys. Elsie thrust the plate holding the cream-filled ginger sponge dusted with icing sugar into Elizabeth's hands and waddled off.

Elizabeth contemplated throwing the sponge at the large retreating flowered arse then she picked up the plate and opened the supper room door.

Sharon Cartwright, almost falling out of low-cut green sateen, came towards her, bearing a fruit and nut loaf. Her gaze flicked over Elizabeth. 'Nice dress.' She narrowed her eyes at the sponge. 'Where are you going with that?'

'I'm taking a piece out to poor old Mr Potter.'

Elizabeth threaded between the groups clustered on the dance floor, passed through the admissions door and gained the enveloping darkness. She placed the plate on the tank stand and stood looking out towards the car park behind the hall, searching for Julie; but she couldn't see the Everetts' car anywhere. '…in the car park, during supper time…' was what they had arranged yesterday evening. The phone was kept in the kitchen so total privacy was impossible. Even though the call had come through when everyone was occupied or outside, Elizabeth thought she heard footsteps on the other side of the door. She had started talking loudly, asking Julie about Rob and what dress she was going to wear.

The wind had started to rise and the few gums left around the cricket ground for shade tangled the moon in black leaves and tossed her back and forth. Elizabeth shivered.

As she turned towards the hall, she almost cannoned into a man coming the other way. 'Sorry,' she mumbled then started when she saw his face.

He gave no response to her surprise; perhaps he was used to this. His presence had certainly caused a commotion in the supper room.

'Who was that?'

'I think he's married to one of Josie's older sisters.' (The Irvings were a family of nine.)

'Oh, it's disgusting! Disgusting!'

Elizabeth caught the sting of some obscure excitement in Elsie Armitage's exclamation, something *sexual*, just as Phyllis, cradling a sheaf of sheet music, entered the supper room.

'Bigotry is the only disgusting thing here, Mrs Armitage.'

'Well, how would you like it if one of your daughters…'

It was times like this when Elizabeth forgave her mother everything: her insistence on dancing lessons, all the fittings for the red taffeta horror at the local dressmaker's, every detail of the pointless fuss and fal-lal involved in nights like this. It was enough to hear her bell-like voice and watch her ascend the three wooden steps to the small platform which passed as a stage, where she seated herself before the piano, spreading out the music for the first number of the second bracket. Phyllis's hair, miraculously untarnished, was coiled neatly at the nape of her neck. She wore a navy blue dress flecked with a small white print, and two artificial white flowers were pinned to the collar. She bent her head over the keys and struck a note so that Louisa Grainger, nestling her violin, could tune. Between them, lame-legged Vince Connelly hoisted his piano accordion onto his lap. A sandy-haired man from a town to the north sat behind twin snare drums. Vince looked at Phyllis, looked at Louisa, that long-necked spinster; he gave a count and they were away.

'Come on, Lizzie, I'll have the first one with you.' Mick seized her and began to steer her expertly across the floor.

It was meant to be a quickstep but Elizabeth turned it into a slow-and-broken-step, tripped once then stumbled again.

'I don't know where you get this from,' Mick mused, while he waited for her to adjust her sandal and the other couples went on around them. 'I've always been a good dancer…your mother and me, when we were courting…'

'Don't want to hear it.' When he started talking like this, Elizabeth glimpsed something fragmentary and glamorous, like light flickering on brocade at the end of a dark corridor. Her parents' lives, before she entered them, were foreign countries where she was forever a stranger.

She drew in her breath and tried to concentrate. She remembered the dance instructor, with her frizzy perm and halitosis, insistently counting but it was no good; Elizabeth couldn't get it right. The music shifted to 'I'll take you home again, Kathleen'.

'Here, Lizzie, I'll have this one.' Chris Petersen, who had been leaning against the wall watching, walked over to claim her for the Pride of Erin.

'Yeah, you take her, mate, you might be able to get a better result...' Mick looked around, spotted Elsie Armitage and whirled her off, despite her protestations of now being 'too old for all this'.

Chris smelt of something sharp and alpine. His dark blond hair curled over the collar of his denim shirt. Elizabeth could just about manage the Pride of Erin, the simple steps forward and back, then the twirl beneath his raised arm. The second time, as his hand dropped to clasp her around the waist, it lightly grazed the side of her breast. Elizabeth caught the middle finger of that hand and bent it back, not far.

Chris swore then laughed as she walked from the floor, ignoring the stares from surrounding couples. 'You're not nearly as much fun as your sister!'

Elizabeth burned red then yellow. She pushed down the bile in her throat and felt the imprint of the hand like a brand. This was all the fault of that slut Michaela, with her overwhelming ambition and lack of regard for others. That *slut*.

Her brother came over as Elizabeth stood with her back to the wall, waiting for her heart to calm. 'What's going on?'

'Nothing...'

It was sometimes unfortunate that Graeme was not as stupid as he looked. She leaned into him and let him lead her, shambling across the floor. She trod on his toes; he trod on hers but it was the Progressive

Barn Dance so they didn't have to torture each other for long. Elizabeth passed along the line of men, circling the hall. She was sweating, sure that she stank (although not as badly as some of her partners, who smelt strongly of the dairy).

After a while, they became a blur: she grunted in response to any attempts at conversation. She only wanted flight, to break free from this tedium, around and around and around, held together by the beat of the piano and the thump of the drums.

Phyllis sat like a queen upon a throne, her forearms inscribing small circular movements as her hands shaped the sound. Briefly her eyes met Elizabeth's; then they turned back to the music.

Chris Petersen was three partners ahead. Elizabeth got ready for another scene because she was not going to dance with him again but then she almost shouted at the top of her voice because, coming through the door with his wife Sandra was lantern-jawed Pete Everett.

The tempo slowed for the first of the up-close ballad numbers. Elizabeth took her chance and dived through the door. She passed the tank stand and grabbed up the patient sponge. In the corner of the car park, out past the toilets beneath the big pine tree, was the Everetts' Holden, the L-plates fixed front and back; there was the pale crepe-de-chine glimmer of Julie.

It had started with a dare about driving lessons. Julie wasn't making good progress with Rob or her father. She had failed her test twice. Elizabeth, who had been able to drive since she was ten, boasted that she could get Julie through the test before the exams started. 'And then we go on a pub crawl and you pay.' What they were doing was illegal because Elizabeth didn't have her licence either but they stuck to the back roads and hardly saw anyone. It had been a time of exploration, of finding strangeness in a landscape taken for granted and thought familiar. Last week they had turned down the lane next to Archie Mathieson's place, which led to a grassy tunnel lined with leaves. Gullies of water squirmy with frog spawn still stippled the paddocks and a scarlet robin sat bright as a spot of blood on barbed wire. They kept going, were worried about getting bogged when the clearing opened abruptly before them, flooded in wintry light. There were the remains of fruit trees: a single gnarled plum still sprouted leaves but the rest were just compost and stumps. Daffodils and snowdrops clumped eccentrically and a tangle of sweet peas twined a briar rose. Further on, they found a rubble of bricks from a chimney and a red camellia gone wild, scratching the sky.

'There must have been a house here once.'

Beside the camellia, their hands had touched, then clasped. They had wandered about, hoping to scavenge something unusual or interesting but had only found pieces of thick crockery and rusting pipe. They had kissed then, Julie more expert.

She quickly disentangled herself, 'Let's get back to the car,' but then had phoned last night, when her parents were late night shopping in town.

Elizabeth slid into the back seat, holding the sponge before her like a conquering hero returning from war with a captive. Julie already had a bottle open although at first all she could do was whinge about Rob, who was still back at the footy pavilion, pissing on with his mates.

'Where is he? I'm so horny I could root the crack of dawn.' Her shoulder made a soft sucking sound against the vinyl seat as she shifted restlessly. She slouched down with her dress spread out over her knees and the bottle resting in her lap.

'He'll be ages yet.' Elizabeth took the bottle and swigged.

Heat veiled the windows, creating a steamy cocoon.

She settled against Julie and felt the blood moving beneath the pink-marbled shoulder. She smelt Lux soap and Charlie perfume. She kissed the shoulder then tore off a piece of the ginger sponge. 'What took you so long?'

'We stopped off to see the Potters.' Julie took the sponge, wiped off the excess cream with a finger then placed it against the red taffeta bodice. 'You know what old Bert's like when he gets going.'

'Yeah, awful old gasbag. Hey, this isn't bad.'

They tore the sponge apart then left the plate with its castle of crumbs on the front passenger seat.

Elizabeth licked icing sugar from the corner of Julie's mouth. She bit her neck. 'Les be friends,' she whispered.

'You're a dirty girl,' slurred Julie, lifting the bottle, but she didn't resist.

It got kicked over and the dregs congealed as they slid down the seat and pashed. Elizabeth tasted the sugary grease of lipstick on malty wetness. She ran her hand over slippery crepe-de-chine and fumbled with tiny buttons. Her own dress twisted around her legs, hobbling her, and she clawed it free. Water trickled down the windows, dissolving the world. She was in a new place where there was only heat, heat and flesh, flesh opening to her beneath her own forcing hand and moans which were suddenly strangled by a looming blue shadow.

Phyllis opened the car door. 'Get out of there!' she hissed.

Elizabeth, high on alcohol, sexual excitement and a sudden rush of oxygen, started to giggle.

Phyllis reached in and slapped her. 'Come on! You don't want people to see you like this!' She dragged her daughter from the car but Elizabeth broke away.

'Leave me alone! Get off me!' She shook out the folds of her crumpled dress then hitched it to her knees and stalked to the toilet. She rearranged her hair as best she could but the make-up was past repair so she wiped it off. She splashed water on her face then looked dazedly around. She felt dislocated: a fissure had opened between what was now and what had been; yet she had to go back. She wet her face again, dried it with the hem of her dress then went outside, to where her mother stood guard.

Elizabeth ignored her and looked around for Julie but the car park was empty and still. As she made her way towards the hall, a group of kids rushed suddenly out of the darkness. Elizabeth recognised Bernie, glassy-eyed, mad from too much sugar and the excitement of staying up past his bedtime.

She caught him to her as he dashed past. 'Don't ever grow up.'

She heard the sound of Scottish reels, the only music the band played without piano accompaniment.

Inside, the floor had cleared, to allow the engaged couple to dance their ceremonial lap before presentation of the gift bought for them by community contribution. Care was taken to ensure that the gifts were both practical and decorative. Crockery was a popular choice, a tea set or some cake plates. Stocky Craig Simpson who drove a refrigerated tanker for the local milk factory came forward to claim his intended and together they circled the hall, smiling but not looking at each other, concentrating on the steps.

Sharon Cartwright came up behind Elizabeth, flipped her hair affectionately then draped her forearms across Elizabeth's shoulders. 'How far gone do you think she is?'

This was a popular question at kitchen teas and Elizabeth assessed Josie's floor-length skirt with a practised eye.

'No more than a couple of months.'

Josie was skinny so she didn't show but the engagement had been announced suddenly so everyone assumed the usual reason.

'She'd do it with anyone!' Sharon hissed. 'Even after she started going with Craig she was still screwing Steve.'

Elizabeth thought of the words 'glass', 'houses' and stones' but she said nothing.

Julie had just come into the hall with Rob. Hair upswept and skilfully clamped, lips filled with carmine, she walked straight past Elizabeth, vivaciously exclaiming a greeting to Val Markham standing in aqua chiffon next to Graeme. Rob gave Graeme a matey punch on the arm. Elizabeth knew better than to wander over uninvited. She would ring Julie tomorrow but she couldn't think that there would be any more driving lessons. She glanced up at Phyllis on the stage but Phyllis was smiling at Michaela, who was deep in conversation with Jamie, one of her horsey mates.

Would her mother talk to Julie's parents? Probably not: that would be admitting that something significant had occurred. Phyllis's sense of propriety and her sense of shame would keep her from making contact.

At least Michaela was away from Chris.

'I rooted him,' Michaela had told her calmly. 'I rooted him,' as though she was reciting a bus timetable. 'He said that if I rooted him he'd let me ride Shiloh in the dressage class at the next show.'

Shiloh was a seventeen-hands-high chestnut thoroughbred gelding, the Petersens' gift to their only child for his eighteenth birthday. Shiloh would be a fitting mount for Michaela.

'But Mich, what if…?'

'It's all right. We used frangers. It was nothing, over before it got started but you mustn't tell anyone.'

Not a chance. If Mick found out, he would feel obliged to knock Chris's head off and then where would they all be?

A strapless bra, limp as a dead fish, lay where it had been kicked beneath a chair. Elizabeth scanned the hall but couldn't see the Aboriginal man anywhere. It had been her mother's hubris, her pride in thinking herself better than these backward yokels, which had made her respond to Elsie Armitage the way she had; nothing more.

'Going for a piss.' Elizabeth edged herself from Sharon's grasp.

Mick always left the station wagon unlocked; *if you can't trust your neighbours who can you trust*? She climbed into the front passenger seat and stretched out her legs. The car held her family: there was the yellow pencil Bernie had been searching for all week, a faint tang of saddle oil which was Mich, the silvery halo of silence surrounding Gerard and fibres of coarse reddish fur which meant Mick had been transporting Bandit in the back, despite Phyllis's rule to the contrary. Elizabeth kicked off her sandals then wriggled out of her pantyhose with their sopping crotch. She flexed her toes and felt the air circulate all the way up. She let her whole body breathe; then she opened the glovebox.

She was disappointed with *Orlando*, particularly given that Miss Foster had recommended it. 'Here, Lizzie, I think you might enjoy this…' Elizabeth couldn't put her finger on it but she felt there was something dishonest about the book, something which dodged the point. It had started well enough with the young boy Orlando adventuring all over the place but she had reached the second part where the boy became a girl who seemed to spend most of the time changing her frock.

Elizabeth read on, her face illumined pale gold by the reflection from the small plastic torch she held. She enjoyed the part where the female Orlando dressed up as a man then went out to meet some pros; once they realised Orlando was a girl they all seemed to have a fairly good time. But then she met Marmaduke Bonthrop Shelmerdine and settled down to have his kid. Bore. Major bore, like the army.

Some of the language was beautiful – *…the glass was green water, and she a mermaid, shining with pearls, a siren in a cave, singing…* – but in the end, the couples in the book were fairly similar to the couples in the community hall.

Elizabeth put the book down and switched on the local Saturday night request show. Elvis walked for a while through cold Kentucky rain; since he died last month, you couldn't turn the radio on without hearing him. 'And we played that for Lee and Wayne, Wendy and Daryl, Julie and Rob and all the gang…' Irritably, Elizabeth turned the dial. There was a lost-woman wail of country and a riff of some kind of classical music then her finger came to rest on a frequency not contactable by day, carrying words of an unknown song which spoke to her of dreaming and wandering. She sat listening until a blast of static obliterated the frequency with a noise like wind through an open door.

Elizabeth switched off the radio. In three days' time, she would take her driving test and pass. The exams were nothing; she would pass them too and then the world would open up. She threw the book away as her mother played 'God Save the Queen' to close the dance. *Orlando* bounced onto a rear armrest then slid down and remained beneath the seat for almost two years. Graeme found it when he was cleaning out the car, getting it ready for sale, after Mick died.

Richard Tauber in a monocle

Elizabeth sat in the lecture theatre listening to Professor Oscar Postlewaite's unctuous Oxbridge drone: '...Eliot remains supreme among the writers of this time and his work, both poetry and criticism, renders him a colossus of twentieth-century literature. Pound and Joyce are, of course, significant figures. Some *feminist* scholars...' Professor Postlewaite paused behind his podium for maximum effect and waited for the titters to subside. 'Some *feminists* have attempted to proselytise on behalf of Virginia Woolf but she remains a minor writer, inhabiting the ethereal mist of her own genteel concerns...'

There was a slap at the back of the theatre, the sound made by a chair seat flipping up as its occupant stood abruptly. Elizabeth wasn't the only one to turn her head.

'Oh dear, oh dear!' boomed Professor Postlewaite. 'I seem to have offended one of the ladies. Come back, my dear, I spoke only in jest!'

There was feeble light in the lecture hall: it played blearily on some soft and subtle fabric and the deep-water phosphorescence of pearls below a flickering helmet of hair. Sun blasted briefly through the open door like an annihilating angel; then she was gone.

'Who's that?' Elizabeth asked a just-waking Alex beside her.

'Some rich bitch who studies art history. She's really up herself.'

For no other reason that she was bored rigid, and because she was irritated that the son of a High Court judge should call someone a 'rich bitch', Elizabeth stood up and followed.

'Oh dear, I seem to have started my own women's movement...'

She made university history by giving Professor Postlewaite the finger then shadowed the blonde across campus as she made her way along a path lined with bare and scrappy poplars. Elizabeth lost her for a moment in the maze of concrete pillars plastered with posters advertising bands and causes then spotted her climbing the steps to the undergraduate library. The blonde paused to push back her windblown hair before she disappeared again. Elizabeth passed through the library entrance hung with the portrait of a long-dead prime minister, just in time to see the pink shirt vanish upstairs.

When she reached the top of the second flight, she felt a small treacherous spurt down one leg but she made sure her quarry was safely seated before heading for the toilet. A red-scrawled *War is menstruation envy!* on the back of the door made her smile as a cramp clutched and squeezed her. Another seized her as she emerged; she leaned dizzily against the wall. The blonde was still there, ensconced behind a glossy-paged art book.

She looked up, raised her eyebrows; then her expression sharpened. 'Are you all right?'

'My period's making me a bit crook, that's all.'

'Well, sit down and stop following me around.' She put the book to one side. 'Would you like a glass of water?'

'Yes…no…okay.'

The blonde departed, returned and Elizabeth sipped slowly from the plastic cup.

'Why didn't you say something?'

'Well, I thought you'd either go away or eventually approach me.'

'No, not that. Why didn't you say something about Virginia Woolf?'

'Oh…' The blonde waved her hand and the light caught the icy point of a diamond on the third finger. 'Men like that thrive on attention. He would only have generated more laughter at my expense then gone on in his smug little universe. Sooner or later Woolf will be recognised as a pioneering genius and be remembered as one long after Professor Postlewaite has retired to grow roses in some dreary suburb. It's better to ignore him and do your own work.'

'Really? And what's that?'

'This.' The blonde turned the book round. 'What do you think?'

Elizabeth stared. She had never seen anything like the women arranged on the shore of the lake. It might have been a scene from some primeval time or perhaps from a time far in the future. They lay draped with voluptuous insouciance on a cloth which also held cups and a coffee pot. The water beckoned orange, mauve and azure while the sky was variegated green and yellow. The grass was stippled red; the hills were purple blots edged with indigo. The women themselves formed a second rainbow. The image was a kaleidoscope: it shattered your eyes then they put it back together again.

'It's…colourful.'

'Colourful!' The blonde snorted. 'I'm sure Matisse would be gratified to hear that.'

'What's it called?'

'*Luxe, calme et volupte*. It means…'

'I know what it means,' said Elizabeth, lying through pain-clenched teeth. Really, the girl was up herself. She glanced at her watch. Right now she should be meeting Renee for coffee to discuss articles for the next edition of the student newspaper. Orgasms were good for cramps: if she was lucky, she would also be able to fit in some late-afternoon sex.

'Well, what do you think about Woolf?' the blonde suddenly asked.

'Me? What would I know?'

'You have the serious look of someone majoring in English.'

'I'm meant to be. I'm taking the honours stream but I hardly ever turn up. Anyway, I've only read *Orlando*.'

'And…?'

'I thought it was a pretty fair effort…' Elizabeth moved towards the stairs, 'but a bit racist, don't you think? You know how it begins with Orlando swiping his sword at the black man's head that's been carted back to England and kept as a trophy. And that image occurs again, towards the end of the novel, I think Woolf actually refers to it as a "nigger's" head…'

'Yes…yes…you're right, she does.' The blonde looked at Elizabeth with sudden, slightly anthropological interest. 'Where are you from?'

'Me? I'm just a scrubber from the bush.'

'The country?'

'Yeah, there. What about yourself?'

'Oh…' The blonde waved her hand. 'All over, really. Russia, originally, but we didn't enjoy that. Then Berlin, which worked out for a while, then not. Here, now.'

'And…' Elizabeth imitated the hand wave, '…you like it here?'

'Oh, yes, we love it.' They looked at each other and laughed. 'Come round to dinner,' said the blonde.

'All right.' It was Annie's turn to cook tonight so that meant some sort of watery concoction featuring lentils. 'Whereabouts are you?'

The blonde named a street in an area Elizabeth had never been; she would have to take the bus. 'I'm Sarah, by the way,' the blonde called after her, as Elizabeth descended the stairs. 'Sarah Rosenthal.'

'I'm…'

'I know who you are. I saw you on television.'

'Oh, well, we all have our fifteen minutes. That was mine. See ya tonight.'

Elizabeth unlocked her bike and rode through suburbs which always made her think of an old song from the sixties, *little boxes on the hillside…and they're all made of ticky tacky…* Twenty minutes later, she turned into a tree-lined cul-de-sac and opened the unlocked front door. A strand of crystals hung in the kitchen window and a poster tacked to the wall proclaimed, 'It starts when you sink in his arms but it ends with your arms in his sink.' Elizabeth stood at this offending item and drank a glass of water while she stared through the window at the Hills hoist which was hung with a pair of pink overalls, a sarong, pairs of King Gee work pants, women's underpants but no bras. Despite the poster's anti-housework message, the place was quite tidy because Annie, that frustrated revolutionary, kept everyone in order with rosters for shopping, cooking and cleaning. Elizabeth placed the glass in the sink, unwashed, then turned to the two letters on the table.

Dear Lizzie

Sorry I haven't written for a while but the last few weeks I've been shit-faced most of the time. Andy and I went out pub crawling Thursday night and didn't get back till 3 in the morning. There was another chick with us but she passed out and when we got her home to our place she chucked all over the carpet so there goes our bond money. The house is a sty at the best of times, the boys never do anything and Chrissy, the hopeless hooer, spends most of her time in bed with Steve.

It was a pretty good turn-out for Dad's send-off and the priest didn't carry on with his mumbo-jumbo for too long. Seemed quite a decent bloke, actually. Ann Petersen was dressed up to the nines but still managed to look like crap, as usual. Overheard her at the wake talking to Thelma Claridge. 'Poor Phyllis, first it's the daughter, now this.' As far as that goes, don't feel too bad, his heart had been shit-house for a while. He could have gone any time. But you've certainly given things here a bit of a stir-up. It's all out in the open now! It's one thing to talk about 'my girlfriend', quite another for the whole country to know you're a leso. Mum told Graeme that you had tarnished the family name. What fucking name? (You know how she's always been about 'maintaining standards.') For a while there, you were doing good, getting accepted into one of best unis in the country, but after this, well, it's name out of the family Bible. Apparently she's been giving everyone at home the silent treatment, just like the good old days, so I'm glad I'm not there. Graeme's still a bit pissed off about the bail money but he'll get over it, says you just need to meet a real man, they're all limp dicks where you are. I told him a hard man is good to find.

Sienna is shaping up well and I should have her ready for the show season here. I took Geronimo upcountry the week before last to some trials. He made a mess of the jumping but got third in dressage, which is not too bad given that his off hock still gives him trouble. Anyway, enough of that. I know you think a horse is something with four legs that eats grass in a paddock. Gotta go. Be good if you could have a few for Dad, sometime. Love on ya

Mich

Elizabeth sat on the bed and reflected that the most popular pastimes in one of the best unis in the country and a small-town ag. college were fairly much the same: drinking, casual sex and missing lectures. She caught the 'too' in her sister's letter which wasn't meant to be ignored. She had tested Michaela's loyalty, tested them all with her behaviour. Briefly she touched her breast, as though she could still feel the bruise where the cop had punched her. Things had got rough at the demonstration; some young bloke, probably an agent provocateur had insisted on antagonising the police. She and Alex had only just been able to prevent the Gay Collective banner from being destroyed. She opened the second letter, which was written in purple biro on half a brown paper bag.

Dear Sis

Today in art class I drew a blue horse and the teacher Miss Sheldrake said there's no such thing as a blue horse and I said, 'What about Franz Marc then? Your stupid,' and she sent me to the Office for the rest of the period. I hate it here, its full of stupid teachers and most of the kids are really dumb too.

Gerard is like a zombie but every day Mrs Claridge gives him a lift into town so he can be with other zombies. I hope I don't end up like that. I'm not going to.

Graeme has started going out with Val Markham, the one with the really big boobs. He says her father's cows have the biggest udders too. I reckon they'll get married. Graeme says he gets tired of having to think about getting a root. At least when your married its there, so I think they'll get married.

How is uni going? I saw you on the telly. Raelene O'Brien from school who is in the same form as me says its disgusting and that God made Adam and Eve but I told her to get stuffed and what would she know. I got sent to the Office because the teacher heard but I don't care. Anyway I'd better go now. Here's a sketch I did last week.

Sincerely
your brother Bernie

Elizabeth smoothed the enclosed page, which featured three parrots sitting on a tree branch. The birds looked both comical and lucid, rather like her brother's letter. It must be lonely for him now that Michaela was gone. Gerard had left school after failing everything at the end of last year and was involved in some sort of dead-end 'job creation' scheme involving horticulture. Graeme no doubt just went on plodding through rain and cow shit. 'It's lovely that these fine old family traditions are kept going,' Elizabeth murmured.

She looked at the clock then got up off the bed and went into the shower, remembering her own times at the office, in front of the small genial headmaster, whose only aim was subjugation. Bernie wouldn't take any notice; he would just keep drawing. She must write back soon.

Sarah, sitting before the heater in the flat her parents paid for, sipped a glass of wine and listened to the stereo. She had changed from her jeans into a dress of amber wool and, while she waited for the farm girl to arrive, she reviewed a day which had not begun well.

She turned the diamond ring once, was about to do it again, caught herself and stopped. The fight – there was no other word for it – with Aaron had surprised them both. It wasn't so bad that there was no way back – no, that certainly wasn't the case – still, much more serious than anything that had ever happened between them. Sarah reached for the copy of *Cosmopolitan* she had picked up impulsively at the supermarket checkout. 'Be a Sex Goddess For Your Man. Lingerie can be pleasing and teasing…'

What garbage! She threw the magazine across the room, then, the result of long training, picked it up and placed it on top of the television. It was difficult to pose as a sex goddess for someone you had known since you were six. She looked across at the photo on the bookcase, 'Well, what would you do?' and, receiving no response, turned the record over and the oven temperature down, hoping that the farm girl wasn't on some hippie vegetarian trip. Sarah smiled. Elizabeth was scruffy and gauche but it had taken courage to follow her through the battery of sniggers in the lecture theatre. There was yearning and sadness behind the freckles and green eyes, as well as intelligence: an intriguing combination.

After another twenty minutes, she turned off the oven and took out a single plate because clearly she would be dining alone. She replaced Warren Zevon on the turntable with music she preferred, just as there was a knock on the door. When she squinted through the peephole, a green orb glared back. She undid the locks.

'You're rather late.'

'So was the bus.' Elizabeth set down a bottle of wine and thrust out the flowers she had managed to collect on her headlong pelt across the campus into town. They were a kind of red lily, some already turning brown at the edges.

Sarah ran water into a dark green vase and they glowed with raffish intensity.

'Are you hungry?'

'I could eat a horse.'

'I'm afraid I've only got a lamb.'

'Lamb's good. We can send out for horse later.'

'You stay here, I won't be a moment.'

Elizabeth stayed but didn't stay put. Her own room was a shit heap in which she spent the least possible time, a compost of unwashed clothes and half-remembered dreams. There was a framed snapshot of two girls, one astride an old brown and white pony, while the other held the bridle. That was all. There were no art deco lamps, no Japanese lacquer vases holding red and yellow tulips on polished coffee tables, no posters for French films. Music like she had never heard issued from the stereo.

The top of the bookcase held clusters of photos depicting decades of weddings, bar mitzvahs and birthdays. There was a shrine-like ambience which made Elizabeth want to sweep them to the carpet but one held her attention, a solitary head-and-shoulders studio portrait, the face all radiant angles, turned in three-quarter profile with an almost raptorial gaze. The back of the photo was stamped in German.

'Who's this?'

'That's my great-aunt Miriam.' Sarah carried two steaming plates from the kitchen. 'Please put it down. It's all we have of her. Her brother, when he died, left it to my father. Glass of wine?'

'That would be good. It was the Nazis…?' Elizabeth braced herself for piles of corpses, blue-tattooed numbers and cattle trucks at night.

'No.' Sarah set out glasses and gestured to the table. 'No, we got out before all that. We saw the writing on the wall and, of course…' she paused as she sat down, 'past a certain time there was quite a lot of writing, on walls, on shopfronts, on synagogues. No, Miriam, she was the black sheep of her family…'

While Elizabeth attacked meat spiced with apricots and pine nuts, Sarah took her back to 1920s Berlin, describing a girl born into a conservative but by that time prosperous family. Spoilt, the only daughter, Daddy's darling, able to do as she pleased but destined for marriage to a worthy bourgeois. 'Then she outraged her parents by having her hair cut short and telling them she wanted to go to university.'

'Shock! Horror!'

'Sure was, but that wasn't the end… No, only the beginning: there had been the job as a journalist on one of the extraordinary number of papers in circulation during the Weimar Republic, and then the lover, who not only wasn't one of us but a communist as well. You can imagine how that went down.'

'So what happened?'

'Well, things were bad in Germany by 1929…'

'They were pretty rat shit everywhere…'

'…and getting worse. Karl, the boyfriend, who was a journalist too, got some sort of posting to the Soviet Union. You know, I've never thought of this but it's possible he was approached by the NKVD. That was…'

'I know what it was,' said Elizabeth, irritably.

'Anyway, that was it. Miriam went with him and they disappeared.' Sarah put her knife and fork down. 'We think that they were gathered up in the purges of the late thirties.' She blotted her lips with a napkin. 'Or possibly, later, in the fifties, when Stalin came down heavily on the Jews.'

Elizabeth, who was already on her third glass of wine, looked at the photo. You could be flesh and blood, held in someone's arms, then one day, all that's left if you're lucky, are lines burnt by light onto paper and kept on the mantelpiece. In the background the tenor sang, *you told me you loved me when we were young some day…*

'This music…' she murmured. 'I don't know…it makes you sad…'

'It's music from that time. Richard Tauber.'

'Never heard of him.'

Sarah handed her the record sleeve. Richard Tauber wore a monocle and a tuxedo. He wore a black silk top hat and a white silk evening scarf. He looked pleased with himself and the world.

'He was Viennese, born illegitimate. His mother was a singer too. He had to leave Austria in 1938…' She disappeared into the kitchen then reappeared with a plate containing dates, strawberries and creamy-yellow cheese. 'Try some of the cheese with a date. It's like eating ice cream.' Elizabeth complied; she now knew, through her association with Alex, that it was not bizarre to serve cheese and fruit at the same time. Then she was caught up in the flow of history again.

'Anyway, Tauber went to England…'

Movement, diaspora, exile: Elizabeth had it in her own blood. Mick had told her about the Great Famine; but these stories were different. Sarah poured dessert wine as Richard Tauber started on the 'Merry Widow' waltz.

'I know this, I know this!' Elizabeth swung tipsily out of her chair. She took a few steps and held her arms around the waist of an imaginary partner then tripped up and collapsed in a heap on the carpet. 'I know it,' she repeated stubbornly. 'You waltz to it.'

'If you can remain upright for long enough, yes.' Sarah set down her glass slightly too hard, causing wine to slop out and stain the cloth. She rose and extended a hand. 'Care to dance?'

'I can't dance.' Elizabeth hung her head. 'I've got two left feet. I'm hopeless.'

'Says who?' Sarah repositioned the turntable arm then grasped her around the waist. There was rough comfort in the flannelette shirt, which was quite unlike anything Aaron ever wore. 'Look it's easy. Just follow me: one, two, three, one, two, three…'

At the sound of the familiar litany, Elizabeth automatically stumbled.

'Careful.' Sarah clutched her more firmly.

They had another go but it was no good.

'Well, let's try it another way. Perhaps you should lead.'

It was such a revolutionary idea that Elizabeth was stunned. 'You're taller,' she muttered.

'Fractionally,' Sarah conceded. 'But it's not working like this. You lead, I'll follow.'

It was like stepping off a precipice; Elizabeth closed her eyes and jumped.

'See, you're a born leader.' Sarah smiled encouragingly.

'Thanks.' Elizabeth held her breath and concentrated…*you are my heart's delight, and where you are, I long to be…* She tried to feel the music with her body.

She felt Sarah, attentive, in her arms. Her spine straightened, her head came up. She attempted a modest twirl.

'Ohh-ahh!' Sarah clutched her in mock alarm. 'I've created a monster.'

Elizabeth merely smiled and jauntily repeated. She managed a circle of the room without bumping into anything. She felt she could go on all night, dancing to Richard Tauber in a monocle. She *was* Richard Tauber in a monocle, suavely romancing nubile frauleins in opera houses across Europe while outside the barbarians clamoured at the gates.

Girls were made to love and kiss / And who am I to interfere with this / Is it well? Who can tell? / But I know the good Lord made it so

She smelt Sarah's scent: sweat, yeast, a subtle and expensive perfume.

Am I ashamed to follow Nature's way? / Shall I be blamed if God has made me gay?

'We'll assume that he's using "gay" in the old-fashioned sense.' Sarah giggled.

'Could be.' Elizabeth leaned over and kissed her on the lips.

Sarah's face went blank.

'Sorry, sorry…' Elizabeth stumbled back.

'It's all right, it's fine, except I think I want to sit down.' Sarah returned to the table. 'It's all right, it's fine.'

'Do you want me to leave?'

'No. No.' Sarah touched her fingers to her lips. She looked slightly dazed.

'I'd better go.' As Elizabeth bent down to retrieve her backpack, Sarah moved towards her; straightening, their faces collided.

'Oh! Oh! Oh, shit!'

Refusing the offer of an ice pack or a lift home, Elizabeth ran across crunching dead leaves, just in time to catch the last bus. She was its only passenger and as she watched her nose visibly ballooning in the dark window, she thought that she would not see Sarah again. Girls like that were curious, wanted a thrill. They got scared when things turned real. Well, her loss; she'd never know what she had missed. Elizabeth groaned, held her throbbing nose and wished for her throbbing cunt to subside as well. She might not have minded so much except that she had given up one of her usual shifts at the supermarket deli so she could spend it dancing drunkenly. The rent was due at the end of the week. Where was she going to get the money from?

Three days later, when Elizabeth was in the student newspaper office with Alex and Renee, Sarah walked in. She wore a cream dress, lipstick and carried a tan leather clutch purse. With her other hand she held up a plastic bag.

'I've got something for you.'

Elizabeth hesitated.

'Oh, well then, if you don't want it…'

Ignoring Renee's snigger, Elizabeth took the bag. Inside was a small fedora with a red and yellow feather in the hatband.

'It's great. Thanks.'

'That's okay. I was in the Salvos yesterday. I thought it was "you".'

It was hard to imagine Sarah surrounded by hippie leftovers and faded Crimplene pantsuits. Elizabeth stroked the feather and put the hat back in the bag.

'You're not going to wear it?'

'Yeah, come on, Lizzie, let's have a fashion parade,' said Renee.

Sarah studied her for a moment then glanced at Elizabeth, taking in the identical cropped hair, army pants and denim jackets.

'You two are so much alike,' she remarked pleasantly. 'You could be cousins.'

Alex laughed, then, seeing the glares directed at him, went back to his cartoon of Lord Mountbatten being blown up the IRA.

'I've got to go,' Sarah said. 'I've got a French language lab in ten minutes.'

'I'll walk over with you…'

Later, when they were sitting in the refectory, Renee took Elizabeth to task. 'Where did you find her? Is she some closet case you picked up in a bar?' Then, after Elizabeth had provided an edited version of events, 'You want to go out with her, don't you? Sarah?'

'Yes,' said Elizabeth, 'I do.' Then, slyly, as she poured sugar into her coffee, 'You sound jealous.'

'I'm *not* jealous. I'm just surprised you want to go out with someone who wears make-up and a skirt. That's what we're fighting against, all that patriarchal role-based shit! Perhaps you better buy yourself a suit and tie!'

Now it was Elizabeth's turn to laugh and she did, until heads turned and Renee pushed her chair in so hard that it fell backwards with a clatter onto the floor.

Elizabeth didn't dress in a suit and tie for her outing with Sarah that evening but she took some trouble, putting on a navy blue pinstriped men's suit jacket and her best pair of jeans. She positioned the hat on the back of her head, tilting it at a jaunty angle then checked herself in the mirror: not Richard Tauber but not too bad. She pushed back the curtains and watched for a blue Holden Gemini, pleased that she didn't need to take the bike or the bus, because the air was chilly. It didn't matter whether *Salon Kitty*, the film Sarah had suggested they see, was any good; Elizabeth wouldn't be paying attention. Afterwards she would try to steer Sarah towards a bar. Alcohol had been helpful the other night; she'd packed a spare pair of undies, just in case.

She reached into her pocket and took out the piece of paper, already creased to fragmentation from being folded and refolded during the last two months. When she had first opened it and seen who it was from, she had expected a thumbnail dipped in tar but there was not one misspelling; her father had always maintained that educational standards when he was young were superior to those of today. ...*I don't care what you do...you'll always be my Lizzie...but there's no need to make such a song and dance about it...think about your mother...* Mick must have been worried about what Phyllis might do but he had been the one who collapsed. Michaela had phoned with the message, 'She doesn't want to see you.'

A few days after that, Elizabeth had borrowed Renee's car and driven up Black Mountain. She parked and sat looking out at the night, thinking about her father's hands, how she couldn't remember ever having seen them without some cut or scratch, the flesh peeled back to reveal the rawness beneath. She drank a toast to him from a bottle of Jack Daniels and recited one of Henry Lawson's poems which had been a favourite of his: ...*you and I were faithful mates all through the roaring days...* As she descended, dry-eyed, she thought Mick would have understood.

Elizabeth folded the sheet of paper and slid it into the drawer of her bedside table, just as a car horn sounded outside. She wouldn't mention the letter to Michaela but she would write to her: *he drank too much and worked too hard.* It seemed an honest enough epitaph.

Elizabeth picked up her backpack. She walked through the silent house and switched on the porch light as Sarah leaned across to open the passenger-side door.

Tuckerbox blues

'Stop here!'

'Here?' Elizabeth's wraparound sunglasses, worn beneath a green-tipped Mohawk, gave her the look of a bulbous-headed insect, blankly staring. 'You sure you want to stop here?'

'Yes, here. It's halfway. It'll be all right for one night.'

The sign out the front of the low, L-shaped, pink building trimmed with grey stucco read 'Tuckerbox Motel'. In the strip of garden set back from the footpath, a few palm trees struggled for survival.

Without waiting for an answer, Sarah got out of the car, slammed the door, and headed for the part of the building marked 'Office'. Elizabeth sighed, took off her shades and followed.

'We'd like a double room, please.'

'A double?' The man behind the reception desk, short, slight and shiny-domed, looked confused. 'You want a room with a double bed?'

'Yes,' said Elizabeth. 'A room with a *double* bed.'

'A double,' repeated the man.

'If it's not too much trouble.' Sarah smiled.

The walls of the office were painted brilliant pink and trimmed with burgundy: surely he could not have had anything to do with it. Elizabeth detected the wishes of some busily managing little woman. She watched Sarah push back the blonde hair other women were always telling her to cut off and smile at him again.

'Is there a room available?'

'Oh, sure, sure!' Tiny beads of water oozed from his forehead as he flipped through the open book on the desk.

'That's the wrong date,' said Sarah, sweetly, pointing. 'It's the nineteenth today.'

'Oh, so it is.' The little man turned back a page. 'Now,' he went on in a businesslike tone, 'you girls want a double.'

'Yes, please.' Sarah smiled. She handed over money and commandeered the keys.

'Well, that was interesting,' she remarked a few minutes later, as Elizabeth dumped the suitcases inside the door.

'Not as interesting as this.' Elizabeth bounced experimentally on the bed clothed in bilious mustard chenille. 'Nice and firm. You want to try?'

'No, thanks.'

'Oh, come on.'

'No!' Sarah took out bottles of Clinique, and an eyeliner pencil, and disappeared into the bathroom. Elizabeth switched on the television; Lady Diana Spencer smiled and waved. She was everywhere at the moment. You couldn't turn round but there she was, simpering over the frog she had kissed. Elizabeth watched for a few minutes, learned that the details of the wedding dress were as closely guarded as a military secret, then changed the channel.

The toilet flushed. Sarah emerged, shiny-faced and kohl-rimmed. She placed the eyeliner in her handbag and started for the door. 'We should find somewhere to eat.'

'It's a bit early to get a feed.'

'I'm hungry.'

Elizabeth groaned and followed. This weekend had been a mistake. The visit to Sydney had been bad enough but then there had been the drive down the highway in the old Holden, the hot air stretched taut by scratchy silences which had forced her off the road into this dusty sheep town, with its streets wrapped in pale autumn light and carrying the scent of tedium. The city had given her a life but this place, with its bleached and anaemic landscape, brought back memories which floated in her mind like islands of bruises or clots of fear.

The car coughed into life and coasted down the hill. Two boys kicked a footy on a vacant lot and the words of Cold Chisel's 'Choirgirl' drifted plaintively on the air.

'Isn't that a song about abortion?'

'I thought it was about drugs.'

'They're a good band. They're massively good, live.' Elizabeth peered through the dirty windscreen as a group of hoons in a hotted-up Monaro drove past, shouting. 'Piss off, you bloody galahs!' She gave them the finger then stopped outside a flat-roofed brown oblong.

The sign out the front read 'Tuckerbox Inn'.

'Will here do?'

'It looks a bit tacky…'

'Well, you can't expect the Ritz in a town like this.'

'…and what's this tuckerbox thing?'

Elizabeth turned and stared. 'It's what the town's famous for: *The dog sat on the tuckerbox…*remember?'

'No.'

'You're joking.'

'No.'

'You're unbelievable.' Elizabeth took the shades off and wiped her forehead. 'I can't believe you don't know. The dog's an Australian icon.'

'Well, I'm very sorry. Obviously an important aspect of my education has been overlooked.' Sarah got out and slammed the car door.

A chalk board on the footpath announced, 'Tonite! The Aviators!' The lounge bar was deserted except for the intermittent bleepings and spittings from a bank of poker machines.

'Is it too early for counter teas?' she called.

'No, love, you're right.' A heavy-busted, middle-aged woman stood behind the bar polishing glasses. 'What'll it be?'

'A middy of Old,' said Elizabeth.

'Do you have Campari and soda?' asked Sarah.

'Campari…what's that, love?'

'It's an Italian wine, sort of pinkish-red, in a tall slender bottle…'

'A tall slender bottle…' said the woman doubtfully. 'No, I don't think we've got it. Just a tick…' She stood perusing the row of bottles along the top shelf of the bar. 'There's ouzo,' she said at last. 'That's Italian, isn't it?'

'Ouzo!' echoed Sarah, rolling her eyes.

'Don't be such a bitch,' whispered Elizabeth. 'She's only trying to help.'

The woman finished her search, picked up a tea towel and wiped her hands. 'No, sorry, love. We haven't got it.'

'Gin, then. Gin and tonic, please.'

While Sarah waited at the bar, Elizabeth strolled to the jukebox. She looked completely at home in this expanse of cheap chairs and mottled carpet but Sarah knew that there had been the mother who, as Elizabeth put it, ruled 'with an iron fist in an iron glove' and who had guarded against any tendency in her children to follow their father's well-worn path to the pub.

Sarah carried the drinks to the table, serenaded by 'The Ballad of Lucy Jordan'. Elizabeth capered a few steps on the dance floor. The spiky green halo of the Mohawk dipped and pierced the air. It pierced Sarah with lust. They had only slept together once at her parents' house and that had been a surreptitious slither between the sheets at three in the morning. She sighed, remembering the recent visit to the North Shore.

Her father had done his best, asking Elizabeth about her part-time job on a community newspaper. 'Well, that sounds very…interesting. Would you ever consider working for a more mainstream publication?'

Her mother, who, when Sarah first left for university, had said, 'Well, even if you don't do anything with your degree, you might meet someone nice,' had spent most of the time assessing Elizabeth's hairstyle, the ripped jeans and flannelette shirt, the five silver rings in one ear unbalanced by the three in the other. Clearly, this was not the son-in-law Rachel had envisaged.

Sarah couldn't tell her about the taste and smell of Elizabeth, the wild wrestling which was a prelude to more complex and delicate games. There had been less and less of those lately and she wanted to know why.

She sipped her drink then lit a cigarette and blew out the smoke as Elizabeth sat down. 'So…what's going on between you and Biscuit?'

'Not a lot.' Elizabeth picked up the coaster advertising a local plumbing business.

'Do you want something to be going on?'

'What do you mean?'

'You *know* what I mean.'

'Well…there is nothing going on.'

'*Biscuit*,' murmured Sarah. 'Jesus, fuck!'

'I know, I know,' agreed Elizabeth, although secretly she quite liked the name and thought it suited its owner.

Biscuit, who had been baptised Anne, had creamy beige skin and hair of a thick wheaten gold. She had several currant-sized beauty marks on her belly. She even had one on her clitoris as Elizabeth had recently discovered. There had been a lot of jokes about eating going around when Biscuit changed her name but she didn't seem to mind. She worked at one of the women's refuges, was good with the kids there and wore floaty, severely out-of-date cheesecloth dresses.

'Oh…' crooned Sarah. 'Sweet Biscuit!'

'Cut it out. Let's order.'

It was over the steak Dianne and grilled flounder with chips that they decided to visit the Dog.

'You really want to go there?'

'Well, it is famous. It is an *Australian icon*.'

'Yeah, all right, don't take the piss.'

'No, I'm serious. I'd like to see it.'

'Yeah, something to laugh about with your colleagues at the gallery. D'you want another one?'

They had another one, then another. By the time they left the Tuckerbox Inn, they were both quite drunk. When she opened the car door, the collection of plastic dinosaurs Elizabeth had blu-tacked to the dashboard lit up eerily. The car lurched forwards then backwards then forwards again.

'We could walk.'

'No, it's on the edge of the town.' Elizabeth dug her nails into the flesh of her other arm; the pain helped her focus as she trundled the Holden onto the highway. A truck big as a ship sailed past and they saw dark eyes in dark faces, pressed behind metal bars.

'*There's a track winding back to an old-fashioned shack…*'

'I don't think there's anything wrong with monogamy,' Sarah said.

'*…along the road to Gundagai…*'

'Lots of people live quite happily with just one other person…'

'*…where my mummy and daddy are waiting for me…*'

'Stop that! What is that?'

'*The Road to Gundagai*, as sung once-upon-a-time by Peter Dawson.'

'Who's he?'

'He was a famous Australian baritone, around in the thirties, forties and fifties…'

'Another icon?'

'Dad had a record of his. He used to play it when he got on the piss. …*so no more will I roam…* Ah, here it is.'

'Oh, it's like a little shrine,' whispered Sarah.

The dog squatted on its sturdy metallic haunches under floodlights which illuminated the inscription from Bango Paterson's poem.

'What kind of dog is it?'

'I think it's meant to be a kelpie.'

'They herd sheep, don't they?'

'Yeah, fantastic dogs.'

Near the statue was a shop advertising all kinds of Tuckerbox merchandise. There was complete silence except for the distant *hoosh* of cars along the highway.

'Let's graffiti it,' said Elizabeth suddenly.

'What?'

'Let's graffiti it!'

'Why? I mean, it's kind of kitsch but quite nice, really. I think we should leave it alone.'

'No, I want to do it!' Elizabeth ran to the car, rummaged in the boot and came back holding a can of spray paint.

'Where'd you get that?'

'I've got all kinds of shit in there.' Actually, it was left over from last week, when she had helped Biscuit make a banner for the rally the refuge workers were attending.

'What about security cameras?'

'This is Gundagai, not Checkpoint Charlie.' Elizabeth climbed over the low mesh fence.

Soon the Dog was covered in a fine red film.

'What'll we write?'

'How about *Die, Doggy, Die?*'

'No, it needs to be something political.'

'*Political?*'

'Yeah, it should say something.'

'We haven't got time. Someone might come!'

'Wait a minute...'

'No, come on!'

In the end, Elizabeth just sprayed *Free Abortions* around the brick base of the statue. She drove off, tyres squealing, hooting with laughter.

'What a stupid thing to write! As though you're ever going to need an abortion!'

'That's not the point.' Elizabeth steered the car down a side street. 'Let's take the long way home. I don't want some country pig picking me up.'

That didn't seem likely. Everything had shut and there was no sound except for some distant barking.

High overhead hung the Southern Cross. Elizabeth looked up and smiled.

Sarah regarded the iconic spangle and wished for its primordial carbon to rain on Elizabeth's head. 'I found the poem from Biscuit,' she murmured. 'The one where she likens your vulva to a ripe mango and your nipples to pearls.'

'You've waited till now to tell me?'

'I've been testing you…waiting to see if you'd tell me.'

'Obviously.'

A tyre nudged the kerb as Elizabeth negotiated a roundabout. She should have cleaned up. She lost track of things because she didn't clean up. She had been hoping to juggle both relationships until she made a decision – if she needed to make one. Biscuit didn't mind, she'd shrugged easily when Elizabeth told her she was involved with someone else; but Sarah was different. Sarah was keen on kids and considered pairing off a natural event which led to them.

Elizabeth's knowledge about that didn't prevent her from making a disastrous suggestion. 'We could have a threesome: you, me, Biscuit…'

'Absolutely not. Three into two doesn't go.'

Elizabeth sighed. 'Why does it have to "go"?'

'Because there has to be balance in life. Balance and order. Without that, there's chaos.'

'There's nothing wrong with a bit of chaos.' Elizabeth wanted some now, or at least escape from the corner into which she was backed. She remembered the chalkboard on the footpath. 'You want to go back to the pub?'

Sarah looked at her for a moment. She was in no mood for a reconciling video and the television was sure to contain more news about the wretched English aristocrats. 'All right.'

They parked down a side street near the pub then walked. By now, the place was packed and pumping. A group of young blokes, wearing flannies and clutching stubbies, stood outside talking. Elizabeth took Sarah's hand and, steeling herself for jeers and sniggers, strode forward. However, apart from some glances at the Mohawk, the boys ignored her.

One old bloke, with a face like a gargoyle, sitting by himself and nursing a beer in the small side bar, peered at her curiously. 'I know what you are, mate,' he informed her. 'You're one of them new-wavers. I seen 'em on the telly.'

Elizabeth held up her hand in what she hoped was a new wave and passed on. She let Sarah go ahead, knowing that her face would part the crowd like the Red Sea. They staked their claim on the last empty table. While Sarah went to the bar – the middle-aged woman had been replaced by several girls wearing off-the-shoulder spandex – Elizabeth sat down, regretting her decision. This place made her think of the past, about people last seen years ago, of being sent to retrieve her father while her mother waited in the car outside. Still, coming here had been her idea; leaving now would mean loss of face. She reached without enthusiasm for the beer set before her.

'Don't fall off your chair,' Sarah sipped at something dark in a tall glass, 'but you have just been referred to as my "boyfriend".' She indicated a girl with a fluffy perm, wearing figure-hugging jeans and a puffy-sleeved crimson blouse, sitting a couple of tables away.

'Oh, really?'

'Yes, as in "Is your boyfriend a roadie with the band?"'

'Oh…' Elizabeth stared at the girl, who smiled flirtatiously then looked away. The band filed onto the tiny stage and the drummer hit the skins experimentally.

'Do you do any Cold Chisel?' called a voice from the back.

'Now I understand their name,' shouted Sarah, above the noise of the opening number.

All four band members wore aviator-style shades as well as long hair and flared jeans.

'Are they anticipating a seventies revival or are they just behind the times?'

Elizabeth nodded but her eyes had wandered from the stage to the girl in the crimson blouse. She caught her eye and grinned. If she was going to be vilified for misbehaviour, she might as well be bad to the bone. She wouldn't speak; her voice would give her away. Elizabeth decided to behave like a real man and communicate solely in gestures and grunts. She rose, approached the table and signed in what she hoped was a courtly way to the dance floor. The girl got up from the table, leaving her handbag to the care of friends, and followed Elizabeth.

Elizabeth kept her movements minimal. She extended one hand and whirled the girl around unsmilingly then extended her other hand, glad this was the type of dancing you did without getting too close. Feeling breasts against her own might come as a shock to her new partner. Elizabeth looked around for Sarah but she had been claimed by a local with an impressive belt buckle and cowboy hat. The Aviators, who were strictly a cover band, shifted into a raunchy blues. Elizabeth ground her hips, threw back her head and yelled. Sweat poured down her ribcage. She threw caution to the wind and stripped down to her singlet. The girl stopped dancing and stared.

'Your nipples are priceless pearls,' Elizabeth shouted, 'your vulva succulent as a ripe mango.'

Then someone grabbed her by the back of the neck. 'What do you think you're doing, freak?'

Elizabeth twisted out of his grasp, just as the band crashed out its final chord. 'And who are you calling a freak, freak?'

He was short, shaven-headed and in his late teens, possibly a recruit having a night off from the nearby army base.

Elizabeth continued, in her pleasantest tone, 'There's no need to run around pissing in a circle. Think I'll contaminate her?'

The boy swung at her just as Sarah grabbed the flannie tied around Elizabeth's waist and pulled her back. 'Excuse us, please.' She held up a quelling hand to Elizabeth's adversary.

He took in the blonde pageboy, lipstick, silk shirt, linen slacks and looked confused.

'Come on,' hissed Sarah and steered Elizabeth off the dance floor.

Someone punched her quite hard on the arm.

'Keep going!'

They were jostled and someone spat but Sarah didn't let go until they were out in the car park. Then she pushed Elizabeth, almost making her fall. 'First there's Biscuit, then you leave me with these rednecks who think that *windmills* are the most fascinating topic of conversation ever, while you go and slut about…' She pushed Elizabeth again. 'It's got to stop, Lizzie!'

'I'm sorry…'

'Sorry doesn't cover it.' Sarah slid behind the wheel of the Holden and held out her hand for the keys. 'On top of everything, you might have got us *both* hurt. He was stupid, drunk and dangerous.'

'Lucky I've got you to look after me, then.'

'Yes, well, not for much longer. I should leave you here.' Sarah put the EH into gear and stalled it. She swore, engaged the clutch and finally kangaroo-hopped out of the car park down the street.

A soft moan, which she mistook for contrition, made her glance across. Elizabeth had slumped down in the seat with her head in her hands.

Driving, however badly she did it, gave Sarah a renewed sense of control and, as they approached the motel, she said, in an exasperated maternal tone, 'You need to grow up. You're getting too old to be a feminist vandal.'

'I know, I know,' Elizabeth murmured. She did feel slightly ashamed of her behaviour – but Sarah's had not been good. She should have come straight out with things. This 'testing', this setting a trap; there was something devious about it, something wheedling and manipulative. Elizabeth wanted to be back in Melbourne, lying on Biscuit's massage table and feeling the benefit of those soothing hands and that clever tongue. Yes, Biscuit would be easier; much.

Elizabeth grinned suddenly. She glanced up through the windscreen. Her own hands beat out a tattoo on the dash as she recalled the raised spots of velvet on Biscuit's belly which followed the formation of the Southern Cross.

boy/bow-tie/flowers

boy

He was at the tag end of the family and his runt status gave him privilege: sometimes, they just forgot he was there. His mother rarely saw him, usually looked right through him, punishing him for daring to squirm up inside.

It was his elder sister who took him in hand, guided the pencil in his fingers to make his name and showed him lines which shaped the world...*look, Bern, here's a cat*...but he was already past her, claiming the pencil and clamouring for coloured ones at Christmas, drawing the faces of father, brothers, sisters. From the earliest time he saw them: the men locked against themselves while his mother listened to the words of a song only she could hear. Different music came through the walls at night from the older girl's radio, long-range yearning for uncharted territory which faded to static when she faced the day. Only his second sister, galloping her red horse, seemed happy.

School was his oasis, that one-room building with the gravel playground and the library with six books. He sat in the shade beneath the gum trees at the perimeter fence and sketched the blur of a kid scooting to third base. He drew the bowl of rosebuds on the teacher's table, the petals opening, withering, dropping like brown shells onto the varnished wood. He drew, to their admiring cries, the faces of Raelene and Brian and Shaz.

On a trip into town, his sister took him to a real library...*look, Bern, lots of books with pictures, see, you like this one?* He felt a shock like a slap. No fairy tale had prepared him for this, no saccharine story of Sleeping Beauty or Cinderella held this world of grief and love, the pale oval of the Virgin's face below her shimmering hair, the Infant clawing at her pleated gown beneath the enfolding cloak and the radiant boys holding flowers. *The lilies rise like white flame into heaven* murmured his sister but her words were just sound in an ugly building. He made out the artist's name: *San-dro Botti-celli*. He took out the book and raided Botticelli.

He raided Cimabue, Durer and Mantegna. He found Leonardo's *Madonna of the Rocks*. He became a vandal (until the local librarian found out). He took scissors from the mantelpiece and rearranged those pictures, sliced them and slashed them, so that the famous Parmigianino, the Virgin's neck emerging from umber murk like a lily-stalk, cradled a Baby hooded in Byzantine glitter. He carved a plump Rubens Infant from its Mother and set it against the cold glory of a jewel-studded van Eyck Queen of Heaven. For a while, they were his child pornography, kept beneath his bed in a small suitcase he had found on a trip to the tip with his father, and pored through late at night, while his brothers snored.

When he was twelve, he put them away. That was the year his sister fled gladly into exile. She sent him occasional bulletins from the city, as well as posters and leaflets: *I am a woman giving birth to myself* – scrawled beneath...*and my mutant offspring* while she started piecing together the puzzle of her life. Her absence left a rough place: in the hour between the time the primary school emptied and the bus carrying the others arrived at the gate, he lay on the bed which had been hers. An old notebook, full of false starts and abortions, had been left wedged between the wall and the bed.

They lived out behind the wheat silos, where the trains ran through the night during harvest time but were silent the rest of the year. In summer, smoke from bushfires dirtied the sky and buried the sun in violet light while flames scorched the ochre earth...

He saw her story, the characters strung across the page with the continuity of a broken fence against the horizon, each pulling away from the others while inexorably linked by tangles of history and obligation. He didn't understand it but he saw it and it stayed with him, all through the years, as his oldest brother married, the younger sister continued to gallop her horse, the mystic middle brother continued his search and that lovely buffoon, his father, died.

The exile sent a letter but didn't attend the funeral; the paper chain between them wrapped him more tightly in her world. *Remember the Botticelli Madonna, well, she looks like that...* He read the whole saga, went on the roller coaster ride through passion, lust, insecurity, betrayal. There was some *bad* poetry about Minerva, *her shining helmet of hair, her golden visionary shield held up boldly...* etc. etc. which even he knew was a strange way to describe a power-dressing assistant curator. He hoped to meet her, the one time he visited the Big Smoke with a school excursion – 'no, she's away at a conference' – so the curator remained a lovely mirage.

He started the painting in his final year of high school, named it *violet light/ochre earth*, just as the letter arrived telling him about the break-up. His sister lost the plot entirely, pages of drunken maunderings...*it's my fault, I rooted around*...but he didn't hear, buried deeply in the painting. He was tired of enduring, tired of the rain, tired of always coming second to Mrs Ada Simpson's accomplished flower studies in watercolours at the local agricultural show; so when his sister, cleaned out on green tea and tofu at an ashram, wrote to him, *you need a broader canvas, kid, you need to look at the big picture...* he told her *I'll get there as soon as I can...*

He knew he was bright but not intellectual and anyway there were no scholarships to art school. For over a year he did what he could: fenced paddocks, picked potatoes and worked on the roads, a chameleon blending with men who talked about footy and beer. They fixed him up with a fuck from a single mother who took money. (He was grateful to her and to them.) He spent the final months hay-carting, the sweat funnelling between his shoulder blades as he carried then stacked the bales. By the end of the summer he had saved enough to buy a beaten-up Renault which he hoped would take him to the city. It broke down on the outskirts and he hitched a lift from a truckie, looking out at the wilderness of the western suburbs as night closed in and the man played Johnny Cash then suggested a stop at a public toilet.

'Sorry, mate, but it's not my scene.'

The bloke dropped him off, with no apparent hard feelings, at an intersection with McDonalds on one corner and an all-night servo on the other.

The sky looked as though it had been licked by a giant neon tongue.

He took a train, then a tram to the seaside suburb his sister had mentioned in a letter *you'd like it there, it's full of scavengers and seagulls...* He heard distant screams from thrill-seekers at Luna Park and spent the first night in a hostel for homeless men, where he woke, soiled and gritty-eyed, feeling like a drifter.

Water swirled in a chipped bowl. Across the street, a girl in pink stood desolate as a cut flower but he ignored her invitation and bought coffee and an egg and bacon roll. There was a mist just lifting, a membrane of dewy light and he caught a tram and coasted down the wide, white, just-waking street. He descended into the mist as the sun appeared. He went, steadily descending, while above were revealed layers of pellucid light.

By the time he reached the bottom of the hill, he was still shrouded but he saw the Matisse palm trees, the black serrated fronds, shapes that a child might make, or a genius, half his guts cut away, assemble while sitting up in bed.

The young artist watched the mist recede, the limpid water steaming beneath the sun's puncturing heat. At the end of a narrow pier a red buoy kissed the horizon. A ship sailed by like a winged creature. He threw the rest of his roll to the seagulls and thought everything would be all right.

He found a share house and a studio and a part-time job. He took what his teachers had to offer and went to parties, listening to empty theories and empty promises. It was at one of these, standing outside alone, that he seemed to hear his sister's voice: *It's not what you know, it's who you know…* It was time to make contacts, time to give Minerva a tingle.

On his way to the public phone box, the girl in the pink dress walked past him with a man. *…motel room…really hanging out…*her sweaty begging face round and white as a deviant moon. He was sweating himself as he pushed in the coins, prepared for excuses or a less civilised rebuff. They had never met but he imagined smoky eye shadow, designer jeans and a Venus flytrap mouth: blonde ambition. His sister had told him about the emerging Cult of Sarah at the gallery, about the faggot in the textile and costume department who had fallen in love with her and suffered. 'She looks like a marshmallow but don't be fooled.'

When he said his name, there was a blank space on the line; then, 'Of course I'd like to meet you. I'm free tomorrow evening.'

bow-tie

Sarah put up her hair as the sun slanted through the windows in sullen topaz strands. She was trying for an elegantly casual look, self-contained but not staid. A French braid was too prissy; it said 'school marm'. In the end she made a messy bundle which she clamped with her grandmother's ornate clasp. She had Rameau playing on the stereo but she turned it off and switched on MTV. A David Bowie clip kept her company as she prepared for the evening ahead.

She was vaguely resentful about having to go out into a blustery Melbourne night but the alternate was cheese on toast and a rerun of *Some Like It Hot*; anyway, braving the weather would stop her endlessly analysing the events of the past few months, as she tended to do when alone.

She switched on the floor lamp in the bedroom and the cone of light illuminated work clothes left strewn across the floor. Sarah collected them methodically, hung up the black suit and threw the underwear and pantyhose into the laundry basket. She pulled on her oldest pair of Levis but dressed them up then called a cab to take her to St Kilda.

While she waited, she moved around the flat, frittering the minutes before she had to go public again. She was plumping up the sofa cushions and delving down behind them for lost change and old theatre tickets, when she drew out the squashed and dishevelled bow-tie.

Sarah stroked the black silk. She had known it was unusual to be attracted to a man because he did exquisite hand sewing. 'It can only end in tears,' a friend had prophesied. Jonathon had worn the bow-tie to a gallery function at which a minor member of the British royal family had been present. He had had trouble tying it, spent twenty minutes fiddling and cursing while he worked on his speech of introduction. In the end, she had tied it for him.

'It looks beautiful,' he said, kissing her. 'So do you.' (She had worn strapless midnight blue satin, spike heels and pearls.)

Their subsequent exertions, after they had arrived back much later in the evening, rather drunk, must have wedged the bow-tie down the back of the sofa.

Outside, the cab beeped its horn. The streets were already dark: yellow cubes and lozenges showed where people had not yet drawn curtains or lowered blinds. Sarah glimpsed a couple chatting over a stove, a woman towelling a toddler dry. She sighed: regardless of her intentions, this sort of night lent itself to thoughts of 'what if…' and 'could have been…' Would it have been all right, married, incredibly compatible, with a tolerant understanding for his affairs on the side? But they would not have been that for Jonathon – 'affairs'; not always, anyway…

After the break-up, she had resigned herself to becoming crankily celibate. She didn't seem to be able to communicate with straight men, even the ones who worked at the gallery. Eventually, she had gone to lesbian bars but the air of repressed anger she found there dismayed her, as did the gargantuan amounts of alcohol consumed by the grim, life-hardened butches for whom she was a glowing target. But perhaps there were compensations for that kind of life: the butches, for all their bravado, were basically monogamous.

The restaurant the boy had nominated sold itself on its ocean view and had a nautical theme; inside there were giant plastic yabbies and plywood ships in bottles. Sarah drank a Campari and soda while she looked out across the wind-quilted water.

After fifteen minutes, she sighed, ground out her second cigarette and glanced at her watch again. She would give him another five. This was just like his sister, who had always kept her waiting. Just as she was picking up her handbag, and thinking of a suitably face-saving excuse for the front-of-house, Sarah saw him through the front window, loping like a dark refracted ghost.

They had never met but she recognised him before he reached the door: tall, with black hair and heavy brows. 'He caught all the Irish genes in the family.' Broad shoulders although he had not quite outgrown adolescent knobbliness; there was still room waiting to be filled out. Skin still slightly knobbly too.

He shook the French-manicured hand she extended, taking in the apricot silk shirt and glitter of amethysts. This had been a mistake: she wouldn't take him seriously, was probably laughing at him now. He slumped into his chair and answered her questions gruffly. Yes, he had been accepted to study at the best place. Yes, he supposed he must have impressed the selection panel. Well, actually he had bribed them. She laughed. He felt himself relax a little.

A waiter came past and offered to light the candle but she waved him away. They grinned at each other across the table.

She suggested wine, 'Or would you prefer beer?'

'I don't drink.'

His words came out a manifesto although Sarah could tell this wasn't intended. She turned down her wineglass, the way she had been taught, remembering stories about his boozing father, the red-hot quarrels late at night and the mother who smouldered for days after, singeing everyone with her unhappiness.

'No, go ahead, don't worry about me…'

'No, really, it's fine.' She poured mineral water for them both, hoping that the lack of alcohol wouldn't be an impediment to the evening, but they managed to get along.

She watched him as they talked: big hands with long fingers, hands that could strangle or arouse with a touch. Was he still a virgin or indeed interested in women at all? (She had read somewhere that being gay ran in families.) She heard herself name-dropping, mentioning the well-known artists she had met. Why was she showing off like this? Irritated, she pushed away the plate of marinara before it was finished and denied herself dessert, drinking coffee while he scoffed down chocolate mousse. When she took out her wallet, he insisted on paying.

'It's all right, I work a couple of days at an art supply shop, it's the least I can do.'

They walked from the beach, across the Esplanade and through the back streets prowled by men in cars. The boy walked along the side of the street nearest the kerb, protecting her. Sarah was amused by this, and touched. It was something she might have expected from her brother's private school-educated friends, not this kid who had grown up on a farm where the nearest shop was five miles away.

He greeted a girl, wearing pink jeans and standing on a corner, by name.

'A friend of yours?' Sarah couldn't help asking.

'Just a neighbour.'

He took out a long, old-fashioned key then swung open the door. Grey concrete walls and floor: it looked as though someone had begun to build it as a warehouse. Naked beams supported an uninsulated roof. There was what her mother would have described as a 'toilet smell' and water on the floor.

'Won't be a moment.' He fetched a black folio, opened it, then stood back.

There were no chairs. Sarah squatted down to look at sketches of horses done on brown paper, in swirls of black ink and aqua and pink pastel.

She stared at the bunched and twisting energy of the massive haunches. 'Your subject matter isn't fashionable,' she murmured.

'Fuck fashionable.' The big hands, dormant on his knees, clenched reflexively, as though squeezing the neck of a prospective critic or would-be dealer.

Sarah smiled and continued her perusal. 'How's your sister?'

'I haven't seen her since I got here. The last I heard, she was having a shitty time working in a women's publishing collective. They spend all their time fighting about things which don't matter, about whether or not it's counter-revolutionary to publish feminist crime novels...'

'And what does she say?'

'She says, "Go ahead and publish them. At least we might make some money."'

Sarah laughed. 'That sounds like her. She has the pragmatism to do well in business, she just lacks the killer instinct. Don't leave it too long to get in contact...'

'I will, eventually, but you've got to cut the umbilical cord sometime.' He gestured in the direction of the studio's far corner. 'The rest are over here.'

There were a group of small portraits which were self-conscious impasto grimaces, but some landscapes he had produced looked more promising. Sarah studied the largest canvas. It was derivative, of course, owing much to Drysdale. She smiled when she saw the title scrawled wetly in the foreground: *violet light ochre earth*. The harsh burnt country depicted was nothing like the fertile green mess from which she knew he originated. The vast smeary sky went back through Impressionism to Turner but the colours were the artist's own, a vortex crushed by its own melancholy weight and which bore down on the figures below. There was a rusty plough, just above his signature, looking like a post-industrial orphan.

Sarah felt a quickening, a recognition of things to come. There was a germ here, or a seed, something which could be either killed or encouraged. 'I'll buy it.'

He named a price she knew was too high and that she knew he knew was too high. For a moment, her great-grandfather's haggling genes rose in her blood, then she demurred. Really, what did it matter?

'Well, now you owe it to me to become famous.'

He looked at her with such hostility that she almost stepped back. She was already familiar with the separation anxiety some artists experienced at the loss of their work; however, she was not prepared when he batted the top of her breasts then abruptly squeezed them. For a moment she didn't understand what he wanted. Jonathon had picked her up and carried her to the bed, like a character from an old-fashioned romantic movie. There had been this element of fantasy and playing in their relationship, something not counterfeit but definitely artificial, so that now it was a relief to lie on the fish-cold floor beneath this boy and open to his large and peremptory cock, to feel her vertebrae crunch as she was ground into the chill cement.

'Sweetheart, baby,' she murmured against him and felt the sudden hot rush of his coming.

When she woke in her own bed on Saturday morning she wondered what would she do if she was pregnant. Afterwards, he had been terse, not meeting her eyes, although she couldn't tell whether this was the result of contempt, shame or indifference. The lack of a phone in the studio meant that she had had to brave the kerb-crawlers while she walked for a taxi, after sharply declining his half-hearted offer to accompany her. She reached home long after midnight and fell into dreams of horses and lilac sand.

There was nothing in the fridge except coffee and flaccid vegetables so she went out for croissants, jam and milk. The wind lifted grit from the streets and leaves shone optimistic early-spring green. Sarah bought the *Age* and the *Australian* at the newsagent where women's magazines gushed news of the latest addition to the British royal family: 'Gorgeous little brother for Wills!' The mother looked flushed and sleepy; the father appeared goofily proud at having achieved what any man took three minutes to do. Sarah winced a little, remembering last night; it was definitely time for a change of scenery. For no reason other than it was possible, she decided to go across town.

She drove up Punt Road with all the windows down and Madonna on the radio, entering the network of working class streets transforming into strips of cafés, galleries and shops. This was the happening area, taking over from washed-up seventies Carlton, the type of place where you might buy retro vinyl (records and clothing) or drink cocktails with names like Orgasm and Deja Vu or see a man wearing a tutu walking along Gertrude Street.

flowers

'Oh, my *de-ah*! Will you look at *that*! That's such a *ba-a-ad* look!' Gloria stood, pointing her wand at the figure looking into the window of the new gallery opposite.

Elizabeth, who had just come out of the florist holding a huge starry bunch of carnations and altamiras, followed the sparks of the rhinestone trajectory. It seemed that the wand could conjure ghosts or long-lost images of desire.

'I'll be right back,' she called, as she crossed over. She was three-quarters of the way there when she changed her mind, but it was too late. Just as she was about to retreat, the face in the plate glass dissolved and Elizabeth was confronted by its fleshy double. 'Are you trying out some sort of New Wave meets Jewish Princess look?' she blurted.

Sarah wore a cream jacket with big puffed sleeves over a denim miniskirt, white tights and red leather ankle boots. Her hair, once a sleek pageboy, had been cut into an asymmetrical wedge which flopped over one eye. A black silk bow-tie was fastened around her neck. 'Tactful as ever, Lizzie. It's good to know you haven't changed.'

'Thanks. Well…what have you been doing, apart from making yourself look like a Duran Duran groupie?'

'I've been living in the present moment. Of course, I shouldn't put that in the past tense. "I'm living in the present moment." How are you?'

'I'm great, yeah, really good.'

'You're full of shit.'

'Oh? You seem very clear about my actual mental and physical state.'

'I've been talking to your brother. He phoned me. We had dinner then went to see his etchings.'

'Did you?' Elizabeth laughed. 'He always was a driven little tyke – although I've been worried about him. I offered to help him settle in, but he was adamant, said he wanted to stand on his own two feet…'

'They seem equal to the challenge. He'll get in touch when he's ready.' Sarah indicated the flowers. 'Getting married? Or are you just the best man?'

'What? Oh, these…' Elizabeth twirled the bouquet. 'Two gay guys I know are having a party. They do it every Saturday arvo at the moment. There's flowers, a pav with strawberries, scones, jam and cream with champagne. Greg dresses up in a tutu and calls himself the Penis Envy Fairy. He goes around with a wand, granting everyone their heart's desire. D'you want to come along?' She proffered the flowers. 'Take these. I can get more.'

'Well, they're rather…bridal.'

'You bridle at them being bridal. I see.'

Elizabeth made to toss them into a nearby bin but Sarah snatched them from her. She had been planning a visit to her brother and sister-in-law later in the afternoon but that could wait. Perhaps the Penis Envy Fairy could grant her most immediate wish, which was to meet no more members of that other family, the Macguires.

'My sister Michaela's down from the bush, just for a visit,' Elizabeth continued. 'It's time to broaden her horizons so I invited her along. I hope she doesn't throw up and disgrace me because it's a civilised gathering, full of refined people.'

'Throwing up's a good way to meet people, sometimes,' Sarah said. 'That's how Sebastian meets Charles in *Brideshead Revisited*. It's possible Michaela will throw up and meet the love of her life.'

They laughed. Without a word, they turned in the same direction. Across the street an orange tram slid to a stop and Gloria flattened down her lavender tulle skirt and climbed aboard.

Elizabeth was looking forward to the afternoon: Sarah would think

Mich was a redneck and Michaela would think Sarah a snotty bitch. They'd hate each other and it would be amusing to see them spar.

'Here, give me that. It looks terrible on you.' Elizabeth took the bow-tie from around Sarah's neck and draped it about her own. She had lost weight and wore a pair of very faded jeans and a pale blue shirt thinly striped with brown. Her hair was back to its normal colour and cut in a very short but stylish way. She flicked the silk around expertly then tightened the ends to make a shape that was jaunty, almost dashing. 'I heard you dumped the boy at the gallery.'

Sarah smiled faintly. 'No wonder you were such a lousy journalist, Lizzie. You never can get your facts right.' But even as she said this, the affair with Jonathon seemed to not matter so much. It was Elizabeth's infidelity which had split them up and after last night, that score was just about settled.

They linked arms and intoned the famous tune from *Lohengrin* as they set off along the street. Sarah grinned at passers-by and flourished the bouquet. How she had missed the fun of Elizabeth!

An old alkie, scrounging in a rubbish bin, scowled at them. 'Cunts,' he muttered, as he shambled off.

'You watch your mouth, you old bastard!'

'Leave him be. You realise his days here are numbered if they keep gentrifying this place. He'll end up in some awful hostel in the outer suburbs.'

At the thought of the outer suburbs, they both shuddered. A faint breath of ozone from the ocean locked behind skyscrapers reached them and light turned the windows of the Greek pastry shop to momentary sheets of gold. Two punks with purple hair went past, looking old-fashioned.

Katherine & Phyllis

Melbourne, September 1951

Katherine O'Connell, sitting in her first-floor residential college room at the University of Melbourne, wears a new suit of Kelly green. Her visiting friend, Phyllis Cameron, is attired in a brown pleated skirt and a dark blue jacket redeemed from dowdiness by the long red scarf draped over it. The college is old; the rooms have wood panelling and diamond-paned windows. Outside there is a spread of viridian and, despite it being only the third day of spring, brisk sunshine.

Phyllis has spent nearly all her money for this week on a dark fruitcake which Katherine is slicing and laying out on plates. They are expecting Bernadette, another friend of Katherine's, who also lives in college. Unlike Katherine and Phyllis, Bernadette is not studying music but majoring in history and literature.

'Where, oh where, can that girl be?' Katherine asks, rhetorically. Bernadette's lateness is legendary. Phyllis says nothing. Bernadette is the daughter of a well-known surgeon. Several times, Phyllis has caught her eyeing the stockings, which Phyllis mends so painstakingly, with a slight smirk. She is glad it is only Katherine and herself. She pours the tea and they settle in for a chat.

One of Katherine's teachers has been hard on her this morning. 'Mrs Tillotson criticised the way I was singing the Schubert. She said I lacked the necessary life experience to give it true feeling. Well, for heaven's sake! What does she expect? I'm only twenty-one!'

They laugh and speculate about Mrs Tillotson's life experience while Phyllis looks admiringly at the shoes Katherine bought yesterday to go with the suit. They're red, with daringly high heels. What would her parents think if she came home to the manse wearing red shoes? She hears her mother's indrawn breath, sees her father's frown. What would they say if she dared to get her ears pierced, like Katherine's? Her mother might mention 'foreigners' but she would never utter the word 'prostitute'. Watching Katherine makes Phyllis feel bold, as though the world is a place where it's worth taking risks.

They agree to book a practice room and meet there the next day. Phyllis will accompany Katherine in the Schubert; perhaps her playing can help Katherine access the song's emotion. Schubert: the genius who died from syphilis at thirty-one. Phyllis shudders slightly.

'Something walking over your grave, dear?' Katherine asks. 'Come on, we need to walk off all that cake.' She squeezes Phyllis's shoulders then rises and takes up her ivory-backed hair brush.

The low-angled sun pours through the diamond panes and patterns the carpet with blue, green and yellow light. Katherine had to work hard to persuade her family to let her live on campus. She wanted somewhere co-educational but her father put his foot down. This college, Catholic and women-only, is the compromise.

'Oh, if the nuns could see me now,' she warbles, securing her dark hair. She twirls before the mirror then takes Phyllis's arm 'Come on, away we go.'

There has been blossom on the trees for a week and the bees hum pinkly as the young women pass beneath the Victorian arches of Old Arts. They leave the university and stroll along Grattan Street, talking and laughing in the sun. A swarthy young man, unloading a lorry outside a grocer's, eyes them with interest.

'Dagoes,' says Katherine disdainfully, looking straight through him. 'Father says we should make them all swim back,' but Phyllis can't think badly of anyone today.

She smiles at the man with the black hair, who whistles slightly through his teeth. Phyllis catches a trace of his sweat when they pass and fire spreads beneath her skin.

Katherine sees this and grins slyly. 'Oh, well, looks as though you've found yourself an admirer,' and they giggle as they cross Swanston Street to the No. 8 tram.

The lights ahead change to green. 'Hurry up, ladies,' the conductor calls good-naturedly, while he waits for them to board. He jerks the cord overhead twice and the city begins to slide by.

Phyllis still thinks of it as a gift; she doesn't believe that she will ever take it for granted, the way Katherine does. Even the shops where she can't afford to buy anything make her feel rich, just because she can gaze into their windows.

When they alight at Collins Street, Katherine takes her arm and they promenade beneath the chestnut trees. They stop outside Georges, the posh department store, but don't go in, even though Katherine's mother has an account there. Phyllis wants to keep moving. She is seized with a sudden restlessness which has something to do with the day, something to do with the young migrant, something to do with the rush of notes beneath her fingers when she plays a Chopin polonaise. She and Katherine cross to the centre of the street and catch the No. 15, which comes all the way from St Kilda beach. Phyllis won't go to St Kilda: she's heard about spivs and pimps. But what lies in the other direction?

'I don't think this is a good idea, darling,' Katherine tells her, as the tram lumbers past Moran & Cato, the grocery emporium on the corner of Brunswick Street and Victoria Parade.

For once, Phyllis ignores her. She watches the houses get smaller and the cars fewer. There are no wide sweeping lawns like those at the university. There's hardly any green, anywhere, just factories and huddled dwellings. The manse is hardly spacious, the largest room is reserved as her father's study where he writes his weekly sermon, but at least her mother keeps a garden which produces vegetables and fresh flowers to adorn the table. What does it mean to live like this, cramped, with no beauty? For the first time, Phyllis notices the tram's few passengers: they are mainly shabbily dressed, middle-aged women.

Impulsively she rises and pulls the cord.

'Oh, must we...?' Katherine trails unhappily along the footpath.

But Phyllis has seen something, a flash of red in this landscape of greys and browns. She moves determinedly back down the street, past a hotel, the smell of which makes her stomach curl ('Drink is the Devil's temptation'), impervious to the man, his face a map of broken veins and lost hope, urinating around the corner.

It is a widespread lampshade in the window which has caught her eye and it is with relief that Katherine says, 'Oh, look, a shop.'

It is a shop, of sorts. The hand-lettered sign in the window advertises, 'Augustus Petronus, pawnbroker and second-hand dealer'. It sounds almost like a name for a Roman legionnaire but the man behind the counter is short with wispy beige hair and pale eyes. He greets them in a heavy accent. He's a New Australian. Behind him, the shop's treasures glimmer like Aladdin's cave.

Phyllis stands awkwardly but she has come too far to turn back. She murmurs, as her mother would, to deflect an unnecessarily intrusive sale assistant, 'We're just looking, thank you,' and surges forward. She makes for the first reassuring thing she sees, a rack of clothes, and reaches in randomly.

Her hand comes out clutching a blouse of midnight-blue moire taffeta. Phyllis holds it in front of her and searches for a mirror. Tentatively she strokes the luscious fabric with her other hand. The buttons on the blouse are mother-of-pearl and glow like moons in the dim light.

'It's lovely,' says Katherine, suddenly appearing behind her. 'Well, go on, try it on. It really suits you. You've got a nice figure and you should show it off.'

Phyllis blushes and thrusts the blouse at her friend. 'It would look much nicer on you, with your colouring.' She turns aside as Katherine takes her suit jacket off and it is then she sees the hatbox, sitting on a shelf between a particularly ugly vase and a watercolour painting of ballet dancers.

Phyllis examines the box curiously. She strokes its round lid, feeling the subtly undulating texture of the leather. She snaps back the hinges and looks inside. There is German writing, of which she can decipher a word or two, pasted on the underside of the lid.

Phyllis feels a lust for possession. The hatbox is large enough to hold her sheet music. The sandwiches, which she makes each morning in Mrs Davy's grudging kitchen then wraps in greaseproof paper, will fit snugly into one of the zippered side pockets, along with a Granny Smith apple. But the box is chic, as well as practical, and will anoint its owner with cachet. Phyllis imagines strolling with it towards the Music building, as the breeze lifts the ends of her red scarf.

Suddenly the proprietor is next to her: 'Hey, you, girl, nice girl, you vant to buy?'

'I'm sorry...' Phyllis's scholarship pays for her tuition, no more. Her part-time job as a telephonist covers her board at Mrs Davy's and her meals and tram fares. The little her parents can spare goes on fruitcake, sheet music and a few clothes.

She smells the pungent breath of the man next to her. She asks him about the writing but he merely shrugs and says, 'It is not my language.' (He recognises it for what it is but he is Lithuanian, someone who collaborated in a minor way with the Nazis when they occupied his country; it is best to be discreet.)

Then Katherine comes over, still holding the blouse. 'Let me.'

'Oh, I couldn't...'

'I insist.' Regally, she pays the man for the hatbox and the blouse.

They re-emerge into the street, Phyllis carrying her prize. They catch the tram to Victoria Parade then change to another which will take them close to the university. However, a few blocks from their destination there is an ominous grinding sound.

'All change, please. This tram not taking passengers.'

'Oh, what a bore,' Katherine says impatiently. 'Come on, let's walk.' She sets off without looking around.

Phyllis hurries to catch her, leaving behind complaints from stranded travellers. She hears threats to contact the local member of parliament and laments about missed appointments but she is also conscious of something ahead, a low rhythmic chanting which is growing stronger. Phyllis, who can hum the bass line from a Bach cantata, strains to make out the words; she catches 'fascist' and 'liberty' then, as she and Katherine turn the corner and see the Trades Hall building, those words are written on the banners which approach from the other side.

Two policemen appear behind them. One looks at Phyllis's red scarf and mouths an obscenity at her. Suddenly there are more police. There are flags red as blood and others which represent various trades union. There are a few other groups present: the Council for Civil Liberties and the Society of Friends.

'Commos!' hisses Katherine. 'This is about the referendum!'

On the twenty-first day of the month, there is to be a vote to decide whether the Communist Party of Australia should become an illegal organisation. Phyllis hasn't thought about it. She's too young to vote, yet here is the issue, right before her eyes. The police move closer and she and Katherine are forced to the edge of the crowd. Someone jostles her and Phyllis feels a shrill of fear. She looks around for Katherine but now there's someone else beside her, a man she recognises.

It's the sandy-haired conductor from the tram which took them into the city earlier, the one who waited for them. 'You girls get out of here. Go back to where you belong.'

He speaks brusquely, almost roughly, but Phyllis senses his concern. Now that her initial shock is over, she sees that the crowd is not very large, less than a hundred people. The police are busy elsewhere; it is quite possible to walk away, so she takes Katherine's hand and leads her to safety. The incident is over almost before it begins. (All she remembers in years to come is that the tram conductor was approaching middle age and had a chipped front tooth and another which was grey.)

As they cross the street, Phyllis feels calm and strong.

Katherine's laugh is a shaky crescendo which fades to a gasp. 'Oh, well, my goodness...That's certainly one for the grandchildren...' then she scowls and removes her hand. 'What a bunch of rabble-rousers!'

'They're only protecting themselves,' Phyllis points out. 'If the referendum succeeds, some of them will become criminals.'

'Well, I should think so! I'm certainly going to vote "yes" now. If I had my way, they'd all be locked up. I'm sure Mr Menzies has the right idea.'

But by the time she is back on her own territory, she has recovered her good humour. A chill has fallen on the air and she switches on the two-bar radiator in her room. Phyllis drapes her scarf cross a chair. She tries not to view it as contaminated; nevertheless, she doesn't think she will wear it again.

'Crumpets!' Katherine announces gaily and while they wait for the crumpets to toast they examine their purchases. 'You'll stay to dinner, dear?' Katherine asks, as she removes the blouse from the hatbox.

'Can't. I have a lesson with Rakowsky, then I have to go to work.'

Katherine pouts. 'Oh, well…' She glances at the lid of the hatbox. 'Let's at least get rid of this tatty old writing and jazz the whole thing up.'

She takes a copy of *Gramophone* as well as some film magazines from a shelf in her cupboard. Phyllis has never seen them before and she is rather surprised that Katherine would buy them. *Movie Life*, *Hollywood* and *Picturegoer* are the sort of thing she associates with the girls who work on the switchboard. She cuts unenthusiastically around photos of Errol Flynn and Gary Cooper. Katherine adds a face taken from *Gramophone*, a young opera singer Phyllis has never heard of, called Maria Callas.

Katherine tells Phyllis that Callas is going to be a big star. 'Voice that can shatter glass at fifty paces, darling.'

They cut and paste while they drink tea and eat crumpets. A few buttery smears end up on the glossy images but Phyllis carefully wipes them clean.

Katherine pastes the last photo, of a blonde starlet, Marilyn Monroe, onto the underside of the lid. She lifts Phyllis's sheet music into the box. 'There, that looks nice, doesn't it?'

Phyllis nods absently as she gazes out the window. She is thinking about the lesson which begins in ten minutes, how she doesn't mind the hair which curls in Professor Rakowsky's nose because he is always offering her something for her music. 'Hand relaxed, hand relaxed, the sound should be as limpid as a glass of clear water...' They will work at the Bach *Prelude and Fugue* while the sun darkens. By the time she finishes, twilight will shroud the buildings and lawns.

A bird with speckled feathers settles on the foliage outside Katherine's window. In the distance, Phyllis hears someone practising the oboe. She watches the starling watching her with its tobacco-brown eyes. She thinks that if she died now, she would be perfectly happy.

A white cockatoo and a pink crustacean

Elizabeth threw the book of baby names across the caravan. Finding it, secreted like an awful embryo beneath the Kombi's mattress as she unpacked, had been the last straw. 'Neutral space': that was what she and Sarah had agreed on before they left St Kilda. The holiday would be a neutral space for them to 'work things through', to 'resolve their differences', to try to find 'common ground', as the counsellor had suggested. But Sarah had cheated by smuggling in this defiant little cargo of anticipation. She made no move to retrieve her contraband, just took an oyster from the plate before her.

For they were yuppies now; Sarah at the art gallery, Elizabeth at the TAFE, and could afford such things. Before they left, they had stocked the Kombi's fridge with expensive cheese, sourdough bread, imported smoked salmon, mangoes and cherries, and two bottles of Moet. Through the window above the sink night bloomed, studded with caravan lights intermittent as jewels in a pawned crown.

Elizabeth picked up the book from where it had landed with its pages splayed. 'Kids clog you up. They clog you up for nine months then they clog you up for the rest of your life.' She had been repeating this mantra since Sarah had made her announcement at breakfast, three weeks ago, completely out of the blue, quite calmly, as though it was the most natural thing in the world.

Elizabeth flicked through the pages. There were a few names she quite liked: Ichabod, Sacheverell, Ugutz. She thought Cerdic had a certain ring. 'Isaiah,' she said. '"God is my salvation". Emmanuel: "God is with us." They're nice traditional names. Or are you thinking of moving with the times? Matthew? Mark? Luke?'

Sarah sighed. She had the air of a bemused parent dealing with a recalcitrant child. Beneath the heavy topaz and agate rings on her right hand, sandwiched between the Brie and antipasto, a group of East German soldiers glared back, aghast that their empire was crumbling.

'It doesn't have to be like this, Lizzie. You could move out. We could live separately for a while, if you're worried about never being able to sleep in again…'

'Bah!' Elizabeth threw the book down.

She reached for an oyster; its iodine tang as it slithered down made her think of dark salty oceans, vast amniotic seas filled with quilled and feathery monsters, nebulous life forms which existed fathoms down, guided only by their own bizarre electric excrescences. The idea of such things made her shudder. Easier to live in the shallows and cling tenaciously to a rock-pool rim washed regularly by warm flutings of foam. She clattered the shell onto a chipped plate taken from one of the cupboards then slammed the caravan door.

'I thought you said you wanted to go for a walk…'

'I'm going for one – on my own!'

They had been arguing when they arrived, too overwrought to realise that the manager had located them thirty metres from the toilet block. Elizabeth flexed her toes in dry grass and set off. The trees clumped around the park's perimeter were darkly sheened by moonlight. Something humped and furry scuttled across the ground and she heard the possum's nocturnal rasp.

Standing beneath the fluorescent strip which showed the grey veins in pale blue tiles, Elizabeth splashed water on her face and stared at her reflection, with its hair shaved to stubble and dyed gold. She groaned and shook her head from side to side then slumped down on the wooden bench. She didn't understand why this had happened; things had been going well. She and Sarah were living the dream, in a renovated 'thirties apartment ten minutes walk from the beach. They had credit cards, a five-hundred-dollar dinner service and a circle of nice friends. They hadn't been able to arrive at agreement about curtain fabric but at least they hadn't reached the stage where they colour coordinated their curtains with their sex toys.

A chubby peroxided teenager in a pink T-shirt stencilled with 'Beach Trash' ran water in a basin and glanced at her suspiciously. Elizabeth wished she could be sixteen again, utterly miserable but with the future an uncharted territory. She waited until the girl left, then trudged across the grass. The sky, matted with stars, promised a perfect day.

Sarah had pulled on the oversize white men's shirt she wore to sleep in and was stretched out on the bed watching the late news. A face filled the screen, bulged, gesticulated then receded into a city square swollen with protesters.

'I put the food in the fridge, if you want some more.'

'No, thanks. I'm stuffed.'

Sarah yawned and clicked the remote; Elizabeth flicked off the bedside lamp. They lay for minutes in amicable truce, watching a satellite wink at three stars through the window.

'You fucken cunt!' It was a low gravelly snarl. There was a moment of silence then, louder, more menacing: 'You fucken cunt!'

'What the...' Elizabeth sat up and groped around for the switch.

'Sshhh! Wait!' Sarah peered through the window. 'It's someone next door,' she reported. 'He's hanging around the caravan next door!'

'I'll get ya, ya cunt,' the voice continued. 'I know what you've done and I know where to find ya!'

A voice within the caravan made an unintelligible reply but Elizabeth caught the words 'mongrel' and 'cuntface'.

'Let's get the manager. This could get nasty.'

'No, I'll speak to him.'

'No, Sarah...' but Sarah had already opened the window and stuck her head out.

There was a barrage of thumping next door.

'Open up, ya cunt!'

'Excuse me, excuse me.' Sarah's hair was loose on her shoulders. She looked like a crumpled seraphim. 'My friend and I are trying to sleep. I wonder if you'd mind just keeping it down. Perhaps you could come back tomorrow.'

'Oh, I'm sorry. Very sorry, missus. I didn't realise that there was anyone there. Beg pardon.'

They heard footsteps retreating. Someone came out of the caravan, muttered something then slammed the door.

'Sometimes those private school vowels are worth every cent your parents spent.'

'I think he was drunk.' Sarah slipped beneath the doona and fitted her hand to Elizabeth's hip. 'Take your clothes off.'

'Don't even think about it.'

'I'm not. You'll just be more comfortable.'

Elizabeth wriggled out of her clothes and pulled her T-shirt over her head. 'Just what we need, a couple of psychos next door.'

'Sleep, Lizzie.'

Elizabeth fell into fractured dreams. She was back in Florence with her brother Bernie, strolling through the Renaissance hallways of the Uffizi but suddenly they dissolved and she was poolside in a banana lounge at David Hockney's place, being served piña coladas by good-looking girls in black bikinis.

But she remembered none of that when she woke to an eggshell-blue sky and a breeze gentle as baby's breath. There was a smell of meat cooking on the grill.

She yawned and stretched. 'I wonder what the poor people are doing today.'

Sarah had bought the papers from the kiosk and they sat outside, eating sausages, bacon, tomatoes and mushrooms. All was quiet in the van next door. The plague was in the news again. Some religious nutter from the Festival of Light maintained it was God's wrath being visited upon Sodom and Gomorrah.

Just as they were wiping their plates with toast, they heard the voice from last night around the other side.

'I know ya in there, Coota, ya fucken mongrel. I'll get ya. I'll blow up ya fucken van…'

'Ya too fucken weak, ya weak prick.'

The door opened. Elizabeth smelt sweat and testosterone; she smelt pathology. Coota wore shades. His skin had a panting, open-pored look. His hair was dark stubble and his blockish frame was dressed in trackie pants and a grey T-shirt. John Laws' voice oozed from a radio behind him: '…now I'm going to tell you about a really good deal, a really great deal from our friends at…'

'G'day.' He turned the radio down and stood with his arms folded, staring.

Elizabeth saw Sarah and herself reflected in the shades like two elongated wraiths.

'Ah, there ya are, ya cunt.' The man who came around the corner of Coota's van looked fifty but might have been forty. He was thin, gaunt as a tree hollowed out by dry rot, and his arms were a kaleidoscope of faded ink. He stopped when he saw Sarah and Elizabeth. 'Oh, beg pardon, ladies. Language and all that. I didn't know youse was there.'

'Good morning.' Sarah held out her hand. 'Sarah. And this is Elizabeth.'

'I'm Ray. This mongrel's Coota. I hope he didn't keep youse awake last night.'

'You're the only thing that would have kept them awake, dickhead.' Coota grinned. His shades sent a flash of white light skywards. 'This silly cunt thinks I've stolen stuff off'er him,' he offered by way of explanation. 'He gets pissed, he comes over to my place and says I've stolen stuff off'er him. He's fucken sick in the head.'

'You're a lyin' cunt,' Ray said doggedly. 'That was a real nice coat I had. I won it at the Traralgon Show a few years back and you took it.'

'I did not, cunt,' answered Coota placidly. 'Hey, girls, I've got something to show you.' He went back into the van.

'Oh, the poor thing!' cried Sarah. 'I bet you'd like to fly away!'

But the cockatoo didn't look sad. It gripped the perch determinedly and surveyed the world with black ironic eyes. A chain the colour of its claws ran between the perch and one leg.

'He couldn't fly very far, love,' Ray told her. 'He's too used to living off the fat of the land. He'd be puffed after fifty metres and then the fox would get him.'

'You could at least let him off the perch!'

'I do, mate.' Cheerfully, Coota hoisted the perch. 'He flies around the van and shits everywhere. Go on, say g'day, mate, tell 'er what ya name is.'

'B'wark!' Regally, the cockatoo unfurled its crest. 'Pretty Boy! Pretty Boy! B'wark!'

'I'll buy him off you!'

'Oh, Jesus, Sarah,' muttered Elizabeth.

'Not for sale, mate!' Coota shouted triumphantly. He returned the cockatoo inside then stood braced in the doorway of his van. 'Would youse like a beer?'

'It's a little early for us.' Elizabeth saw that Sarah had been about to accept. 'We're off to the beach for a while.'

'Oh, *are* we?'

'Yes, and we're taking a picnic lunch.'

'Oh, well, I'll just go and slip into something a little easier to slip out of.'

'Youse ladies are together?' Ray asked, while they waited.

'Yes,' said Elizabeth shortly.

'Oh, well, yeah, fair enough.'

Sarah reappeared, wearing a white cotton skirt and a long sheer aquamarine shirt. Shell-shaped earrings dangled almost to her shoulders and a gold chain fine as a silk thread clasped one ankle.

'Isn't she pretty?' Ray said admiringly.

'Yes.' As usual, next to Sarah, Elizabeth felt like a big old cowgirl. She didn't mind Ray paying court, though if it had been Coota, she would have wanted to punch him.

Coota turned up the radio. '…now I don't agree with everything the Reverend Nile says but where AIDS is concerned, there have been lapses of responsibility, lapses of morality…' John Laws boomed. As the Kombi trundled out of the park, his voice counterpointed the rise and fall of the squabbling at the van.

'I'll fucken drop ya, ya cunt. I'll blow ya fucken van up.'

'Ah, ya nothing but piss and wind, ya weak prick!'

'What do you think it's all about? Do they really hate each other or is it just for show?'

'Neither.' Sarah rested her elbow on the open window and accelerated like a hoon. 'It's a ritual, an acting out, a kind of contained male aggression, like a footy match.'

'You've got an answer for everything.'

'You asked.'

The Kombi, which really belonged to Elizabeth's brother Gerard, thrust its ponderous, fridge-like body into the sparkly air, sailed past a line of wetsuits strung across a veranda like a row of decapitated rubber corpses, and headed for the beach. Elizabeth shuffled through the miscellaneous tape collection and they drove along listening to Jimmy Buffet's *White Sports Coat and a Pink Crustacean*. *'She had some nice ones, oh, what a pair…but they don't dance like Carman no more, no more…'*

'For a twenty-five-year-old, your brother has fucking weird taste in music,' muttered Sarah. 'Why isn't he listening to hip hop or house?'

Elizabeth didn't reply. Jimmy Buffet's rockabilly sea shanties suited her fine as the Kombi climbed around the hills to the beach. On one corner a splintery grey skeleton stood, partially clad in a fibro skin. Sheets of rain-dulled crimson tin formed a haphazard carapace and a pile of planks lay in long grass. 'Someone's dream got stranded.' Surfers slid down waves wind-whipped to glassy peaks and next to the car park a prim wooden building hosted a large sign. 'Hell: Eternity Without Jesus'. No, they had it all wrong; it was merely eternity with John Laws.

Sarah cut the engine. Elizabeth stowed necessary items in a backpack and together they descended the ramp ranged with signs about dangerous undertows and sandbars. A woman ploughed across the beach, yanking a whining toddler toward the row of cars.

'I want to go in the water!'

'Well, you can't!'

Elizabeth opened her mouth then shut it again. She glanced at Sarah, who was impervious, scanning the sand for her collection. Into the plastic bag she carried went a pale grey shell fragment, gleaming black and red pebbles taken from the ocean's swill, another shell, fan-shaped and banded in sienna and cream, then a seabird's feather adrift on the tidal residue of a rock pool and a small cuttlefish stained the pink of a dawning summer sky. She rejected all Elizabeth's attempted contributions until she presented the shard of pale blue glass, its lethal edges smoothed and rounded by the sea. It glinted at the top of the pile, a tamed industrial arrowhead. Sarah set the bag down on the sand and fanned herself.

Far out, barely visible through a light pall of sea mist, a ship threaded the horizon.

'Do you know there's a harbour in Vladivostok full of sea glass?' Sarah held the chip in her hand then threw it up where it burst the sun into splinters of greenish-blue light. 'There was a glassworks there in the nineteenth century which used to dump its refuse into the ocean. It's still there, a whole harbour of glass. The tide carries it out then sweeps it back in again.'

'Yeah?' Elizabeth passed her the plastic bottle of Evian. 'It must look insane underwater. Do people go diving there?'

'It's probably a bit cold to go diving at Vladivostok.'

'Probably difficult to obtain scuba gear, too.'

Elizabeth swigged water and contemplated the ship's possible destinations. Over the last five years she had learned quite a bit about geography because Sarah's family moved around. A man left a nineteenth-century village on a night filled with screaming and flames and made his way to Odessa. He crossed water and arrived in Berlin, where he prospered but his children did not. Boats carried the sons to Sydney, Vancouver and New York, while the man's rebel daughter disappeared with her communist lover into the Soviet Union. The sons' children embedded in adopted soil but lived near harbours, raising families while they watched the sea

Her own history was different: you packed a picnic lunch and lay in the sun then stumbled to the Holden half-stunned and drove home, saying what a beaut day it had been.

She watched the waves pound, regular as pulsing blood. 'You're not going to give up on this, are you?'

'No,' said Sarah. 'I'm going to have a child.'

'We drove for six shitty hours so you could tell me that? Home would have done.'

'Home's full of stuff: your work, my work, our friends, the ongoing commitment we have to the AIDS Help Line et cetera, et cetera. Anyway, I thought this might change you.'

Elizabeth looked to the horizon but the ship had passed from view. What frail islands people were, huddling together while they waited for their ships to come in.

'I pretty much brought up my youngest brother…'

'I know…'

'Yes, but you don't know why. After my sister Georgia died, my mother became very depressed. Bernie was meant to be another girl but when he wasn't…'

'Oh, the poor kid. That must have been awful for him.'

'It was. Terrible. Later, when I was a teenager, Mum had a breakdown…'

'You've never told me that.'

'There's lots of things I haven't told you. Even before the breakdown, she was often off her head. Having kids, losing them, can do that to you. She'd walk around the house for three days without speaking to anyone and when you'd try to communicate, she'd scream at you.'

'Oh.' Sarah seemed genuinely perplexed. 'How can you walk around for three days without speaking to anyone?'

'Believe me, it's possible.'

The hot sand knifed Elizabeth's feet as she stood. She hadn't bothered to bring a hat or bathers and the sun had its claws in her head. She stripped down to her dingy Target bra and knickers and ran into the surf. She gasped as explosions of foam slapped her belly and thighs.

It was a late spring day but the water was cold. She gritted her teeth and thrust her head under. For a few moments, she flounced around in the shallows, waving at Sarah and shouting at her to come in; then she pushed towards the smudged cobalt line at the horizon. She put one foot out but the sand shelved beneath it and the sea, swiftly, treacherously, took her.

Elizabeth was swept down into a crazy cathedral of light and turned as indifferently as a piece of flotsam until her lungs lined with fire. She thrust her arms out, groping, but the muscular channel of water hurled her along then sucked her under. She broke the surface then was pushed down again, pinned by the ocean until she tasted sand and her flesh grazed rocks. The water held her, no matter how she struggled and fought, releasing her occasionally for a suck of air then ramming her down again. When all her strength was used, she relinquished her will to the water and prepared to die. There were seconds of darkness, the sea turned her contemptuously for a final time and she lay, boneless and shuddering, against the sand.

She blacked out again, vomited salt water then breathed. When she was able to turn her head, she saw that she had washed up at the mouth of an inlet. The tide was coming in; if it had been going the other way, she would have drowned. A bloody weal ran down one shin and there was a raw scrape across her belly. Elizabeth lay face down, head turned, breathing brackish air, her nostrils filled with a dank reedy smell. Past the inlet, the ocean was an innocent azure sheet against which a seabird lazily flapped its wings.

It would be nice to fly away. There wasn't anything left for her. Her work was a joke, teaching Non-fiction Writing and Introduction to Research to bored teenagers who were only at TAFE because their VCE marks hadn't allowed them into uni. She would have to move out of the apartment and start on the group house treadmill again. Elizabeth moaned and clenched her fingers into grey sand.

The sun had begun its scalding work on her neck and shoulders. She must stand up; when she tried, her legs gave way. The reeds nearby would be cool although no doubt full of insects. She thought she could hear traffic noise. She started crawling.

She was thirsty. Occasionally her stomach heaved but there was nothing left. She crawled through the reeds and was bitten by mosquitoes and stung by gnats.

Ahead was a clearing where the sand was marked by a circle of stones ringing charred wood and crushed aluminium cans. Kids probably came there to park and smoke; there were empty KFC cartons and other rubbish lying around. She tried her legs again and stood there, swaying, as the Kombi rumbled up and Sarah thrashed her way through the reeds. By the time she reached Elizabeth, the white skirt was flecked with blood.

'Fucking things.' She swatted dispassionately then shouldered Elizabeth's weight.

Together they lurched towards the Kombi.

'Fluids.' Sarah produced the water from Elizabeth's backpack then reached for the first aid kit.

Elizabeth felt the cooling balm of calamine lotion. She realised that she was ravenous, reached into the tiny fridge and demolished a piece of sourdough and Stilton.

Sarah sat on the bed and fed her oysters. 'You pulled this whole stunt just so you could have a good-looking woman feed you crustacea.'

'Actually, I don't think oysters are.'

'Not crustacea?'

'No, they're something else.'

'Really? Poor Lizzie, you've always been a bit of a crustacean.' Sarah stroked the gold stubble then reached into the fridge for the bag of cherries. She drew the curtains then settled back, the juice bleeding, staining her mouth.

Elizabeth leaned over and traced the mouth with her finger. 'Who are you going to get the stuff from?'

'I thought I'd ask Aaron. Old time's sake.'

'Oh, right.'

He was the geologist Sarah had been engaged to when she and Elizabeth first met. He'd got over his broken heart and the last they heard, was extracting bauxite in Queensland.

'You could go the whole hog, get married.'

'No need to be ethnically offensive, Lizzie. No, I won't be getting married. You've changed that for me.'

Elizabeth felt a surge of virile satisfaction. 'That will piss Mozzie and Rach off, big time.'

'Mum will be so grateful to have a grandchild she won't care. And she'll talk Dad round.'

'You seem to have it entirely organised.'

Elizabeth indicated the oysters and Sarah passed the plate. She would look beautiful pregnant, with a big swollen belly and engorged breasts crowned with heavy dark nipples. Elizabeth waited until the oyster slid down. She lifted the skirt and dropped a line of kisses to the reddish-gold pubic hair. 'Pink crustacean,' she whispered. She daubed Sarah's thighs with calamine lotion. A near-death experience didn't make you see fields of white light or hear voices from the other side; it just made you extremely horny. She settled between those pink-smeared thighs but Sarah's arms, sinewy from hours in the gym, pulled her up. She cradled Elizabeth. She rocked her. She rocked her harder and harder then she turned her and rode her into the storm of her coming.

'Quick, oh quick, now!'

Elizabeth knelt above her, shaping her hand around those panting cries. She entered Sarah, slowly, until her whole hand was washed with salty juice. She drove her whole fist, gently at first, into that spongy cavern, then faster and faster until Sarah writhed on the cusp of pleasure and pain. Elizabeth wanted to hurt her. She wanted to turn Sarah inside out and make her grovel and cry but Sarah closed around her, clamped her like a red velvet sea anemone devouring food and carried them both into tranquil sunlit shoals where fleets of silver minnows darted. They kissed, their salt-puckered lips singing mermaid tales of passion and risk then Elizabeth lay with her head against Sarah's breasts.

'How did she die?'

'Who?'

'Your sister.'

'I don't know. We were never told.' By 'we', Elizabeth was referring to herself and Graeme, her older brother and her younger siblings, Michaela and Gerard, as well as Bernie.

Something caught at her memory, the wife of her father's employer, Mrs Petersen, running up the drive, her mouth red like a clown's. Elizabeth pushed it back then kissed the tiny glass of champagne tattooed at the top of Sarah's left breast.

'Enough.'

They slept, curled together like ship-wrecked survivors.

The tide turned. It collected all the detritus of the day and pushed it out to sea. The waves lapped the sand placidly while the rip, that deadly rush of water, carried its cargo of empty bottles, innumerable plastic bags, the body of a feral cat run down by a car load of teenage drunks and an amethyst ring thrown into the shallows by a woman married for thirty-five years.

Sometime during this, Sarah woke momentarily. 'Not on my own,' she muttered thickly, as the few clouds turned to Rococo puffballs and the pleasure craft headed for home; then she slept again.

A petrel's call nudged Elizabeth to consciousness. She struggled up and pushed back the curtain. It was that strange hour when the sun and the moon were in the same sky, the time when things change shape. Elizabeth thought that if she blinked a few times she might get a glimpse of her own destiny but all she saw were reeds black as flags and a fin of corrugated iron serrating nearby grass. She remembered the bottles of Moet in the caravan fridge. 'Let's go home.'

They squabbled over the music, one wanting Bach, the other

Hunters and Collectors, then they discovered that Gerard's tape collection contained neither so they settled for early Joni Mitchell.

The oysters had gone clammy and oozy-looking. They threw them out and stopped off for fish and chips. Elizabeth sat waiting against a lurid turquoise wall, listening to the Vietnamese family at the fryers communicate in two languages. She was reminded of some Friday nights from her childhood, when, in token recognition of her husband's lapsed Catholicism, her mother would treat the whole family at the takeaway five miles down the road. The Vietnamese family would have been in another country, backing the losing side in a war which was nobody's business but their own. Yet here they were: history was a capricious old bitch who made fools of most people.

'Tea.' She tossed the big steamy parcel up to Sarah in the passenger seat.

The wan overhead light illuminated her fragile collection and briefly Elizabeth touched the broken shell, the cuttlefish and the pebbles dulled now to charcoal and beige. Only Sarah could make something whole from a collection of broken things. Elizabeth picked up the pale grey shell fragment, a shattered chamber, pierced and drilled by the ocean. You could see right through to its empty heart, yet something had lived there once. She would miss these small things: the theatre of the dashboard, the long blonde hairs ornamenting the shower door, the art books propped next to the phone, the bed and the toilet. She knew that there would be other, more serious losses but she chose not to think about them just yet. She could just about cope if she focused on the small ones.

When they got back to the caravan park, the windows of the van next door were blank. Pretty Boy sat slouched on his perch outside.

'Look at you, you poor bugger.' Sarah unclipped his chain and cuddled him awake.

'Bwark,' he muttered sleepily.

'Yeah, just hang on a minute, mate.' Elizabeth popped the cork and they sat up in bed companionably, watching the news and feeding the cockatoo chips.

A young man in badly-fitting acid wash jeans took a sledgehammer to the Berlin Wall, watched from both sides by soldiers. Crowds of people around the Brandenburg Gate cheered, drank and danced. There was graffiti, shot from the Western side: *Hier endet die Freiheit,* under which some cynic had scrawled, *von Kapitalism.*

'You'll be able to go back soon.' Elizabeth switched off the telly then broke off a piece of flake. 'They'll open all those countries up to the *freiheit* of *Kapitalism.* You'll be able to find out what really happened to Miriam.'

'Maybe it's too long ago.'

'You'll find out.' Elizabeth raised her Durex tumbler of Moet. 'Let's drink to it.'

They drank. A shadow quiet as a sigh moved past their window; it was just a grey ripple in the air. Then there was a tangerine flash and an anguished screeching of feathers as Coota's van exploded.

Two roses in a hatbox

After lunch, when they were all sitting around the table at Graeme's, Michaela mentioned Julie.

'She's getting a divorce. Good on her. He was rooting around for years.'

'Michaela!' Graeme's wife, Val, said warningly but it was all right, the kids were outside, even though it was at least thirty-five in the shade.

Val's pudding, heavy on the suet, light on the brandy, sat slowly digesting in Elizabeth's stomach. A single fan stirred the air sluggishly. All the tawdry excesses of Christmas, torn wrapping paper and leftover food, littered the table. The noise the kids made, swarming in the cubby, formed a robust counterpoint to the ticking of the truly ghastly, fake eighteenth-century clock Elizabeth had received from Graeme and Val.

'She should have known what she was letting herself in for.' Graeme emptied the last of a celebratory Crown lager into his glass.

Michaela snorted. 'What, so it's her fault that he couldn't keep it in his pants?' She looked across at Elizabeth. 'You should go out and see her. She's bought a place about twenty minutes away. She and her daughter are there. I ran into her a few weeks ago at a Rural Women's Initiative Forum and she looked as though she was having a hard time.'

Elizabeth wasn't particularly interested, although she knew a bit about hard times. After she broke up with Sarah, she went completely off the rails: drank too much; had a disastrous affair. Once or twice, after dark, she sat in her car outside Sarah's girlfriend's place and contemplated tyre slashing. But she had never told Michaela any of this.

She picked up the red plastic reindeer spewed from a shredded cracker. 'I'm sure there's counselling available, even around here.'

'Anyway, you can't go now,' said Val. 'Both my brothers and their families are coming over for arvo tea. They're all dying to meet you.'

Elizabeth imagined moon-faced farmers who voted National and talked about butterfat prices. She tucked Michaela and Brian's gift, a useful if generic book voucher, into her wallet as she got to her feet. 'Julie and I were good friends once.' She caught a small grin on Brian's face as Michaela followed her outside.

They stood beneath the great willow outside the house where the Petersens had once lived and which now belonged to their brother. Heat rose from the paddocks in steady golden drifts. Half a kilometre away, the windows of the small yellow weatherboard were blank and bare. Since they emptied it three days ago, the sisters had barely spoken. They didn't keep much: Michaela took the collection of vinyl LPs, the Johnny Cash and Jim Reeves which were Mick's; she still had the hatbox in her ute tray. Elizabeth took some stuff to the Salvos and the rest to the tip.

She wanted to heal the breach which had opened between them. Michaela's face was gaunt; there were lines around her mouth like parentheses carved in stone. Phyllis took a long time to die: there were journeys to and from the hospital, then a brief rallying, a few days at home before the readmission and final descent. Now, Michaela behaved as though she has passed a test: she had been a good daughter. Elizabeth sensed a certain amount of subterranean resentment that would continue to fester, unless brought to the surface. During the last week, Michaela had attacked her over absolutely stupid things, such as sending inappropriate flowers to the funeral (mauve tulips!) or failing to provide a contribution to Christmas lunch.

Despite telling herself not to be intimidated, Elizabeth found herself resorting to banalities. 'You're having Simon and Tim down for a few days?'

'The monsters? Yeah, they'll arrive tomorrow evening, run riot around the horses and generally make a shit-load of work for us.'

Elizabeth laughed dutifully, although she had met Brian's teenage sons and knew they weren't that bad. They would probably make themselves quite useful around the small stud Michaela and her partner owned.

Michaela took out a cigarette – she had started smoking again – lit it, then stubbed out the match carefully against the tree trunk. It was the season of potential tragedy, of fire and accidents. Yesterday the older boy, Andrew, found a tiger snake curled like a rubber joke on the tank stand. Its striped skin had charred beneath the sun, pinned to the roof of the cubby house, until Graeme warned his children that this would attract more snakes.

'I got a card from Sarah, a couple of weeks ago.'

'Yeah? She does like to observe these goyish festivals, in her own way. I suppose mine will be waiting for me at home.'

'It was nice, nothing Christmassy. Just a picture of her and the bub and the girlfriend, whatshername.'

'Ange. She's a tennis coach.'

Michaela laughed. 'A *tennis* coach. That doesn't sound like Sarah.'

'Ange has very good legs.'

Elizabeth paused to consider the unlikely connections people forge. Michaela and Sarah hit it off, right from the moment Elizabeth introduced them, years ago, at a party in Fitzroy and, since then, had always kept in touch. When Sarah and Ange went to the States last year, just before the pregnancy, Sarah sent Michaela a beautiful fringed suede jacket from Sante Fe, with an accompanying card: 'To my favourite cowgirl'.

Michaela ground out her cigarette then picked up the butt. 'She looks good, Sarah. She's put on a bit of weight but she looks…radiant.'

'Oh, yes, radiant, radiant. Radiant as any Huggies commercial.'

'Well, you'll have to shape up and stop being cynical. You're a godmother now. It's a responsible position.'

'Yeah, well, no one else would take the gig.'

'You'll be a wicked fairy godmother, waving your bloody wand around.' Michaela looked at her watch. 'You better get going. The cockies will be here soon.'

Elizabeth, already regretting her decision and hoping Julie wouldn't be at home, whistled to Beryl, the blue bitch panting in the shade. They set off with both the front windows down and Beryl lying on a damp towel. 'Good girl. If all else fails, I'll use you as a conversational safety net.'

Most people were willing to make small talk about a dog. Perhaps it was similar to the phenomenon Sarah had recently described: 'You'll be walking down the street pushing the stroller and women you've never seen, who would ordinarily pass you by, stop and ask you about the baby.' The universal appeal of babies and pets: Elizabeth let out a short laugh.

She travelled the dirt road with Beryl through open farmland which the sun flayed with light and where overhanging branches provided straggly shade. The harvest had finished recently. Elizabeth remembered how it once was, teams of sweating men hauling rectangular bales into trucks and carting them to sheds but it was all different now and the hay sat on blonde stubble in great golden coils. Green polythene covers were sometimes used as protection and here and there had escaped and flapped, placenta-sad, from barbed wire.

The dirt road became a narrow strip of bitumen then merged with the highway. As Elizabeth approached the town, she saw a group of Asian tourists stopped at the side of the road, photographing Friesian calves. She imagined her father making a joke then talking about his older brother who didn't survive in Changi. This place, unvisited for so long, held memories that stretched back to a time before her birth.

She reached the house on the corner of a small curving side street and saw two galahs pecking listlessly at a nature strip stippled pale green and beige by summer water restrictions. On the front porch a woman sat at one of the ugly metal table and chair sets sold by budget garden stores. She wore a large straw hat and had a newspaper open before her.

It was sixteen years since she had seen Julie; Elizabeth didn't know what to expect. She stood there, thinking she should have brought something, mince pies or a box of shortbread from Safeway, until the woman glanced up. She still looked good although she was almost as thin as the pencil on the table. Her clothes were fragile, white cotton and pale blue silk, but her gaze was assessing.

'Five letters, fourth letter's "m": smell.'

'Aroma,' said Elizabeth.

The woman pencilled it in. 'Outdoor sporting facility, second letter's "r".'

'Track.'

'No. Useless. Won't work.'

Elizabeth thought for a moment. 'Arena.'

The woman wrote without comment. 'Anger. Seven letters. Third one's "t", the last one's "e".'

'Outrage. Your aroma outraged me at the arena.'

Julie smiled quizzically. 'You always were a smart-ass. You better get out of the sun.'

'I've got my dog in the car…'

'Well, you can't leave her there.'

As they liberated Beryl into the backyard, a child came out of the house. Not really a child: she had tiny breasts and translucent skin. She had Julie's fair hair but instead of being neatly cropped it hung to her shoulders, held back by a piece of pretty trash.

'This is Greta,' said Julie.

'Hi there, I'm Elizabeth,'

The girl mumbled and retreated, slamming the door.

'She's being a pain in the arse, sulking because I didn't buy her a Labrador puppy for Christmas.'

'Oh, well, perhaps Beryl will cheer her up. And it must be hard for her…' Elizabeth stopped.

'Knowing that her father prefers to spend time with a twenty-five-year-old in a Spandex miniskirt? Yeah, it's hard. Would you like a drink?'

'If you're having one.'

'Oh, I'm having one. Definitely. Come in.'

They took wine and sat out on the small enclosed back veranda, where plants in terracotta pots gasped for air. Julie had one glass quickly, then another.

Elizabeth recognised a certain bitter recklessness in this behaviour; however, the alcohol helped erode formality. Over the next hour, as the level of the bottle sank, Julie told her story.

She married Chris when she was twenty-one and had Greta almost immediately. She got bored with her job as the manager of the New Image Boutique and, while she waited for the second baby, started a degree in media studies at the nearby campus. The second baby didn't happen but by the time Julie was reconciled to this she was writing her PhD. She began teaching at the same campus even before the farm was sold and she and Chris moved into town. She had recently co-authored a textbook for use in secondary colleges, was active in the district's Film Appreciation Society and had taken up squash.

Almost defiantly, she told Elizabeth that she had quite a few friends. 'And the house keeps me busy. I'm going to extend the garden. And there's Greta, of course.'

'And what's she planning to do with her life?'

'Greta? She's very interested in computers. She came home the other day going on and on about something called the information superhighway. Apparently, we're all going to be moving along it quite soon. She's only in primary school but she says she wants to be a systems analyst!'

'Better than wanting to be a supermodel. Anyway, plenty of time for her to make up her mind.'

'I tell her that. I say, "Go to uni or be a hairdresser, I don't mind."'

'That's a good attitude.' Elizabeth poured them each another glass.

By the time Greta was at uni, it would be another century, a new millennium.

Elizabeth's own future looked increasingly precarious. Her last employment was with one of the television networks, as part of a team which wrote scripts for a hospital drama. The money was fantastic, more than she had ever earned, but the series rated poorly. Elizabeth took what she had saved and went travelling around Australia. (Her brother, Gerard, had become a Buddhist monk; he didn't need his Kombi any more.) At the moment she had an application in the works for a position (with an attendant abysmal salary) as a scriptwriter with the national broadcaster but if it didn't come through, she would be forced onto social security for a while.

She set the bottle down.

Julie leaned back and regarded her enquiringly. 'And you? I seemed to have talked a lot, although I've left out the really good bits about Chris and Cyndi the Slut. What about you? You never found anyone?'

'I did…for a while,' replied Elizabeth, slowly. 'She and I…' she registered Julie's look when she heard the pronoun, '…oh, I don't know, it's a long story…'

'It often is.'

Julie seemed anxious to leave the subject so Elizabeth, perversely, persevered. 'We're friends now. It took us a while but we got there. She and her partner have just had a little girl, Miriam Sophia.'

'Mmm. Nice. And what about your family? I still see Mich occasionally. She seems happy.'

'Mich is happy anywhere there's a horse.' Elizabeth sensed Julie's relief: how reassured by happiness people were.

They went on to discuss Graeme and Val and the kids, their perfectly acceptable and pragmatic lives; then they moved on to Bernie. Julie knew all about his success, had even gone to his last exhibition, the one which took him away to study in Italy.

'And that's where he met Christina. They're married, got a little girl and another baby on the way.'

More happiness. Elizabeth had to admit that even Gerard's austere, shaven-headed choice appeared to have brought him the same thing, although Gerard didn't really exist any more: as well as giving away everything he owned, he had also taken a new name. Elizabeth speculated about a genetic connection between his vows of poverty and celibacy and those of the priests and nuns on her father's side of the family.

Julie laughed. Her face was flushed. The bottle was almost empty. 'I always liked your dad.'

'He was a nice bloke.'

'I'm sorry about your mother. I read about it in the paper. Sorry, I should have said something earlier.'

'That's all right. Anyway, condolences don't really apply. She was a strange and difficult woman and I never knew her very well.'

Julie sipped then squinted thoughtfully into the sun. 'It's true that she never really seemed to fit in here but I thought the two of you got along all right.'

'No. She never accepted my...' Elizabeth's tongue began to wrap itself evasively around 'lifestyle'; then it changed course, '... my sexuality. It was something to do with her background. It was a different time, then.'

'But you kept in touch?'

'Only tangentially, through Graeme and Mich, and she died while I was travelling in WA so I wasn't able to see her.'

'Oh...' Julie had tears in her eyes. 'Well, I think that's sad.'

'It was too hard. I got involved with women when I was young and knew it was right for me.' Elizabeth looked at her. 'Don't you remember?'

'No...what are you talking about?' Julie looked confused then her face stained. 'Oh...that.' She picked up the bottle and shook the last drizzle into her glass. 'That was just a bit of fooling around.'

'Not for me.' Elizabeth remembered the smoky moon above the badly lit car park. 'In fact...' she paused, realisation suddenly dawning, 'it's really where my adult life began.'

Julie twisted the gold band she still wore. 'I've never been able to forget your mother's face. What's that really famous painting by the neurotic Norwegian? *The Shriek*?'

'*The Scream*.' Elizabeth hadn't kept company with an art gallery curator for seven years for nothing. She imitated Edvard Munch's iconic contortion and this set them laughing until Julie reached for the Kleenex.

'I bet you still can't dance.'

'I dance quite well, actually. I can even tango,' Elizabeth replied. She and Sarah had been a hit at one Women's Ball, she in a tux, Sarah in a fringed and beaded flapper's dress. 'All I had to do was find the right partners.'

'I did tell Chris about us, later.'

'I bet he loved it.'

'He did. A few times, when things were really bad between us…' Julie bit her lip. Tears started to her eyes again but she blinked them back. 'He used to suggest we get a threesome happening. He always left the third party unspecified but now I realise he must have had his current fuck in mind.'

Elizabeth didn't know what to say. She wanted to put her arms around Julie but knew it wouldn't be wanted. She wanted to buy more alcohol and she was about to suggest it, quite forgetting that the only pub in town would be closed, when there was the sound of a car in the driveway.

Michaela, driving the old blue Kingswood ute, held her bathers in one hand and waved them like a flag through the open window. 'Come on, you dags, get in!'

'Where are you going? It's getting late…'

'No, Jules, come on! I've packed some leftovers, all sorts of goodies! I know a place just for us, so grab your togs and let's get going!'

'I haven't got any…'

'I've brought a pair for you, Lizzie! Come on, grab the kid and let's go!'

Julie looked at Elizabeth, who shrugged, picked up the paper and leafed through it idly while Julie went to collect Greta. It was a thinner edition than usual but still carried a selection of classifieds. Wedged in between Maureen wanting to sell fox terrier puppies and Jim offering reasonable rates for insulation, she saw an advertisement for the New Year's Eve dance at the local hall: Kenny Bright and his All-Star Band, 60-40. Ladies, a plate please. She pointed it out to Michaela.

'Yeah, some things never change. Do you want to take my car or yours?'

'Better take yours. I think the radiator's gunna boil in mine.' Elizabeth was driving a gold Torana, a real shit-box but it was all she could afford after she left the Kombi eternally stalled on a beach in Broome when the gearbox seized.

'Someone will have to go in the back with Beryl.'

Greta, her barely pubescent midriff gleaming in a tiny knitted top was delighted with this idea. 'Me, me, me!' she crowed.

'No, Greta, it's too dangerous,' said Julie.

'But I want to!'

'No! You'll fall out and kill yourself!' Julie shouted and Elizabeth glimpsed the fear, the total, all-consuming terror that being a mother involved.

'It's on a back road. I'll drive really slowly. It's not far,' said Michaela, and Greta regarded her with interest. Here was an older person who might be fun.

'We could go in yours,' said Elizabeth to Julie, trying to be helpful.

'No, I've lent it…oh, all right!' Julie shouted. 'Get in the back! See if I care! Just don't try to pat the bloody dog!'

'I'm not stupid,' said Greta with dignity.

So love could let go, get past its own self-interest and deliver a child into risk-taking maturity: some people would have considered Julie foolhardy. Elizabeth wondered what she would have done in the same situation and couldn't say. She thought of Sarah with her daughter, radiant, and felt suddenly like an empty seed pod, a dry creek bed running into dust.

The smell from a hundred barbies hung in the air as they set off.

'Rosemary, Frank, Colin, Merle,' Greta chanted because the streets in this part of town were named for the children of a long-dead pioneer.

On the radio, some fallen star from the seventies was mutilating 'Silent Night'. Elizabeth hoped that old Mrs Bates, her neighbour, would remember to collect the mail and feed Pretty Boy, the cockatoo. She lived alone now and quite liked her solitude: it meant you could put your boots on your own sofa even though having to pay the rent alone ensured that the sofa came from St Vinnies.

When Kamahl began 'Mary's Boy Child', she switched the radio off. A light citrusy perfume rose from Julie on her left.

They had reached the web of dusty roads leading to the river. Michaela manoeuvred the ute through potholes. Behind them, Greta bounced and shrieked.

'Stupid kid,' muttered Julie. 'Just like her father, always showing off.'

'Are we there yet? Are we there?' screamed Greta.

'Almost, sweetie,' Michaela called.

They passed between two sentinel gums so close together that their leaves brushed the sides of the ute. The track dipped to axle-deep ruts which Michaela steered around adroitly, swearing quietly, and then the river opened before them.

'Shall we gather at the river where bright angel feet have trod?' sang Julie and Elizabeth looked at her in surprise. It was an old hymn she could remember Phyllis playing on the piano. 'Church,' said Julie, and Elizabeth recalled the fibro building with plain glass windows, tiny as a tractor shed, out in the middle of nowhere, where the Baptists worshipped.

'Was it full body immersion?'

'You betcha.'

They all pelted down to the water. There was much pushing and splashing, a lot of yipping and toes sinking into oozing mud. In the end, Greta was the only one who bothered with bathers.

'You're rude, rude old ladies,' she said, modestly donning a black one-piece slashed above the thighs with pink panels. Elizabeth lay on her back and floated. She heard Beryl scurrying after rabbits and felt the weight of fatigue lift. Her hair fanned out limply as river weed.

After a while, Michaela bumped against her. 'You ready for some tucker?'

'Jeez, Mich, you've really done a good job with this,' Julie remarked, as she spread the tablecloth.

There was cold chook, some kind of stuffed turkey roll, ham, sausage rolls, small spinach tarts, leftover plum pudding with a carton of Coles brandy custard and an array of fruit. They ate until they quivered with food then lay on the ground, swatting mosquitoes.

Elizabeth stretched. She felt the tickle of dried grass then her hands grazed Julie's and linked companionably. Greta fed Beryl and entertained them all with intermittent snatches of 'Jingle Bells' then disappeared for a few minutes.

When she returned, she was dragging the hatbox. 'Look at this! Isn't it cool?'

Julie raised herself on an elbow. 'Greta, that's not yours to be mucking around with.'

'Oh, let her go.' Michaela waved a torpid hand. 'I should do something instead of carting it around everywhere.'

'So can I open it?'

'If you like.'

One of the lid's hinges gave easily but the other remained stubbornly rusted shut. Eventually Michaela hauled herself to her feet and went for the toolbox. Using a large screwdriver, she attacked the resisting lock.

'Here…' Elizabeth took the screwdriver and probed patiently. 'I don't even know why we're bothering.'

'Because it's forbidden. Remember what Mum always said…', and together they recited, '"What's in the hatbox does not concern you"!'

The lock flew open. There was a musty smell of decaying paper and cloth which Elizabeth always associated with university libraries. The hatbox's lining, a pale silky grey fabric patterned with tiny darker birds, had frayed in places, and the pictures of movie stars inside the lid were faded. Otherwise the box looked as it must have when Phyllis bought it.

'Cool!' Greta peered down avariciously.

'Just stand back, sweetheart.' Julie's hand restrained her, giving Michaela and Elizabeth room to squat down and exhume the contents.

A blue and white shawl which had belonged to Phyllis's grandmother lay at the bottom, neatly folded.

'You can have that.' Elizabeth fastened it around Michaela, sarong-style. 'Not quite the way they used to be worn in County Armagh but still quite fetching.'

There was also an ancient silvery envelope, thin as tissue, containing three gold sovereigns.

'Feel the weight of these!' Michaela handed them to Greta. 'Like lead!'

'There's something else.' Elizabeth extracted a folded piece of paper covered in faded copperplate. She smoothed it out and read, 'God so loved the World that He gave His only Begotten Son, saying "Whosoever Believes in me shall not perish but shall have Everlasting Life." Probably some relative of Mum's.'

'There was an old auntie she sometimes talked about, Jane, a deaf old spinster. She used to sit on the veranda when Mum was growing up, writing letters and reading the Bible. Mum mentioned once that the old girl was the only one in her family who talked to her after she married Dad.'

'At least someone practised what they preached.' Elizabeth replaced the steadfast little envelope in the box.

They found a certificate recording the marriage between Michael Francis Macguire, farm labourer, and Phyllis Jane Cameron, spinster.

Michaela stared at it interrogatively. 'What month was Graeme born?'

'April.'

'And they were married in September, only seven months before. Oh, Dad, you sly old dog!'

'Looks like the good Reverend got the shotgun out.' Elizabeth slapped at a plundering mozzie. She picked up the brown-spotted certificate. 'It certainly explains a few things.'

'Such as?'

'Why she always behaved as though her marriage was a cage. Why she always blamed us for lost opportunities.' Elizabeth replaced the certificate and rummaged further. She found a sheet of paper with a Conservatorium of Music letterhead which told them that Phyllis had achieved Distinction for Piano Performance and Credit for Composition.

'I always thought it was the kid's death that sent her round the bend,' murmured Michaela. 'But perhaps you're right… Abortion would have been out of the question, then…maybe out of the question anyway, for someone like her. But, on the other hand,' she continued thoughtfully, 'we can't be sure that she didn't get pregnant on purpose. Perhaps she thought it was a better option than continuing as a domestic slave.'

'Wouldn't she have picked someone with better prospects?'

'I think her father scared all those blokes off. He didn't want her to marry anyone. No, I reckon she got herself up the duff on purpose, just to get away from the old bastard.'

'Oh, girls!' Julie was clearly entertained by these genealogical speculations but nevertheless felt she had to defend the official past. 'Your parents seemed to get on all right. I thought your father adored her, actually, although it was hard to know what your mother ever thought about anything.'

Elizabeth laughed. She rose and rubbed the blood back into her legs. 'She never mentioned any of this to us. She saw it as a stigma, something to keep quiet about.'

'It *was* a stigma, back then.' Julie walked to her discarded clothing and began to dress. 'I remember once when I was a kid, driving somewhere with Mum and suddenly she lets out this little shriek of horror. "I've come out without my engagement ring! People will think I had to get married!"'

They all laughed. The rest of the stuff was about the young Macguires. There was an Infant Welfare Centre booklet detailing gains in length and weight for Elizabeth Katherine Macguire and a booklet for each of her siblings. There were birth certificates and school reports as well as early birthday cards. There were only two cards for Georgia Joy. One contained a clipped lock of blonde hair.

'Do you remember her?' Michaela asked. 'I can't, not really.'

'I only remember that she cried all the time.'

'She had something wrong with her stomach. She wouldn't have survived, no matter what the doctors did. Mum told me, not long before she died.'

'Ah...' For years now, Elizabeth had known that only a child or a primitive would believe you could wish someone to death; nevertheless, at Michaela's words it was as if some phantom, something she had never quite been able to glimpse, no matter how quickly she turned around, slunk quietly away. The sound she heard could have been a tear in the ether closing; or perhaps the first bird making its way home to roost.

Whatever it was, it upset Greta. She frowned, shivered then pounced abruptly on the two remaining items in the hatbox. She ran in a wide circle, shrieking wildly and holding them to her budding breasts.

'She's gone mad,' groaned Julie. 'Come here, you feral child.'

Greta finally stopped before them, panting and glassy-eyed. She sat down with a spine-crunching jolt, legs apart. Her hair fell in a sweaty curtain across her face as she threw the faded brown rosettes into the hatbox.

'What are these?' Michaela picked them up, looking puzzled.

'They're part of the bouquet Mum carried on the day of the funeral. She pressed them that evening. You were asleep.' Elizabeth remembered clamping hands, being carried outside as she howled beneath a vast judging sky.

Tentatively, Julie touched Georgia Joy's photo. 'Poor little mite.'

Elizabeth shrugged. 'It all happened a long time ago.'

So much of life is blighted hopes and broken promises and nostalgia is a waste of time. She could have come home, before Phyllis died. She almost did; but what would have been the point? Something had broken between them that could not be fixed; it could have only been inexpertly mended by bad faith and self-deception. Some mornings, just as she woke, the moment before her conscious mind entered her body, Elizabeth heard the rain falling in shrouds and magpies carolling beneath an early spring moon; but this was as close as she came to regret.

She emptied the hatbox then picked up the desiccated roses and placed them on top. Michaela, Julie and Greta watched as she proceeded with great ceremony towards the river. She waded in until she was thigh-deep. She sat the hatbox lightly on the water. For a moment it threatened to capsize but then the current took it and it sailed away, a study little coracle heading for the open sea. The water twisted it around a bend, out of sight. Julie and Greta, not knowing what else to do, clapped and cheered.

'Well!' said Michaela. 'Well!' She walked over to Elizabeth and placed a hand on her shoulder.

Elizabeth turned her head. She looked into her sister's eyes then suddenly, out of nowhere, kissed her. They laughed, looked away, embarrassed as boys.

'You could come back here,' said Michaela. She glanced at the other woman and her child. 'There's plenty for you here.'

'Nah,' said Elizabeth. She affected a macho drawl. 'Babe, I gotta keep movin'. People don't stay in one place any more. That's the difference between our generation and Mum's.'

'That's true. Even Graeme and Val took time from the milking for a package tour of Canada.'

They gathered up their history and stored it in a plastic Safeway bag. They packed away the denuded picnic – Beryl had nosed off a loose lid and scoffed all the sausage rolls – and Julie handed Elizabeth her trousers. Elizabeth bowed deeply; Julie smiled. She grabbed Elizabeth's hand and swung her around. Elizabeth threw down the trousers and pivoted on her toes. Their clasped hands became a conduit of energy that anchored them to the ground as they whirled and strained against each other. They stretched each other out, their bodies a wheel of blurred flesh then Elizabeth snapped Julie to her and clasped her waist. They strutted, pacing up and down like tigers in the jungle. They ogled each other stylishly then glanced archly away. Julie's head rested against Elizabeth's shoulder; their breath mingled as they raced across dry grass crackling with dead leaves. They only separated when Elizabeth placed her city-soft instep on a twig and winced with pain.

She caught Greta's look. Greta wasn't too sure about this. She was full of anticipation, she would have liked to join in but if Elizabeth had asked her to dance, jokingly, good-naturedly, Greta would have shrunk away. Someone else would have to ask her, another time.

Elizabeth picked up her trousers. She was suddenly exhausted and would have liked a good cry but Michaela was putting the stuff back in the ute.

'Come on, you lot! Time to go home!' She moved economically and purposefully, unfolding the tarp in the back, fastening it around the sides but leaving a space for Beryl.

Michaela would never dance the tango but she would always be delineated by a lean astringent grace. Elizabeth imagined her back on her sixty hectares, amicably directing Brian's sons while she swept a brush through her stallion's tail, surrounded by certainty and love.

'Look at her, the bitch,' she said to Julie. 'Still as skinny as ever.'

'You're not that bad,' said Julie, which caused Elizabeth to busy herself putting her pants on.

They heard the call of the southern boobook and a rustle in the grass nearby.

'A snake!' cried Greta.

'Sweetheart, snakes don't come out at night.'

'They do! In very hot weather, tiger snakes will hunt at night! We learned it in Nature Study!'

'I think Nature's worn you out.' Julie slid along the seat next to Elizabeth and cuddled her petulant child onto her lap.

Greta fell asleep, her head lolling back on her mother's arm stretched along the window.

It was a very clear night with a sickle moon. The Milky Way cradled a million stars. As the ute's headlights bored yellow tunnels into the darkness and spotlit reddish kamikaze waves of insects, Michaela struggled briefly with the column shift. Her elbow nudged Elizabeth and then they trundled through obscuring dust along the first track.

Elizabeth shifted restlessly against Greta's intruding knees, suddenly wanting to be somewhere else. It seemed to her that she had spent all her adult life moving and that if she counted up the kilometres they would probably stretch to the Milky Way. She knew she was in the red zone: she was down to her last few dollars and her last bagful of courage; but she wasn't beaten yet. She sat silently between her sister and her old friend as their faces aligned against the darkness which would disappear and return again and again. Above her, the moon showed sharp as a scythe, a bone-white arc which held the shadowy golden sphere; the promise of the big fat orb it would become. A proton-fine gold border hemmed the sphere, as though someone had taken a cosmic Magic Marker and beaded a luminescent outline, faint and defiant as possibility.

Elizabeth attends a gay wedding in Gippsland

Elizabeth had taken a room at the Union Club Hotel on the corner of the main street while she stayed briefly in a depressed and depressing town in south-east Victoria. She saw the article in the local paper when she was in the milk bar, buying chocolate for herself and a can of Pal for Beryl 2. Then she saw the photo.

Marilyn had not changed much: her hair had more grey and her waist, backside and thighs now carried a menopausal cushioning but she was still recognisably the woman Elizabeth had known almost twenty years ago. She bought the paper and sat on the single bed, reading the article.

There was going to be a police presence at the 'wedding' because various Christian groups had announced their opinion. Elizabeth sat and gazed out the window to the main street below: the usual miscellany of shops stretched up the hill but straight across the street from the hotel was the small park where the ceremony would take place. She had a choice: she could watch it from the comfort and privacy of her room or she could descend and co-mingle in a display of Sapphic solidarity.

Elizabeth lay on her back and looked at the ceiling. So Marilyn had come back to this place which she said she would never visit or live in again. When they had been briefly lovers, Elizabeth had asked Marilyn why she never went home, even though her mother had recently moved into supported accommodation, due to diabetes and a bad heart. All Marilyn had said was 'My brother lives there.'

They had been lying on the bed drinking bourbon mixed with Coke. They did a lot of that, drinking; in fact, it was how they passed most of the day. Elizabeth had become used to waking up in her clothes, with a yellow-green taste in her mouth. Usually she and Marilyn started late morning, around eleven, although Marilyn sometimes started earlier. It was bourbon, Scotch or Bundaberg rum, always mixed with Coke and often followed, when the spirits ran out, by beer. Elizabeth had gained kilos: she sat on the bed next to Marilyn, watching television with her jeans undone.

'Easy access,' Marilyn would slur but she wasn't very interested in sex and, when it did happen, she always kept her upper garments on. Elizabeth didn't discuss it or argue about it with Marilyn, although they got into plenty of other arguments, for no reason at all. One afternoon they had a tussle over the remote control; it was a choice between *The Young and the Restless* and a rerun of an episode of *Doctors and Nurses*. Elizabeth pinned Marilyn's arms above her head with one hand then punched the pillow, next to her head, with the other. Marilyn had lain limp and passive but the next time it happened she had punched Elizabeth back, punched her hard enough to leave a bruise.

Elizabeth looked at the paper again. She hoped that Marilyn was not given to punching her bride-to-be. She took paper and a biro from her overnight bag and wrote to her friend Sarah: *You remember Marilyn, don't you? When you met her, you made unkind allusions to her lack of education. Later you told me she looked like a 'truck driver' and a 'diesel'. You said that I had 'really outdone myself' this time. Well, surprise, surprise…* Elizabeth went on to tell Sarah about the planned ceremony. *Needless to say, I will be well-positioned, ready and waiting to catch the bouquet…* She described the town to Sarah and also detailed her activities there.

Why are these timber towns always so irredeemably redneck? It seems to be so. Here, the trees reach up to the sky and blot out what light there is; this place, at least at this time of the year, appears perpetually enshrouded. The men drive around in big utes with stickers on the back that say, Greens Tell Lies. *The women hang on to life through their kids who leave, as soon as they can, if they've got any way out at all. The rest stay and work in the timber yards or at supermarket checkouts.*

The workshop went quite well. There were the usual suspects: a group of women in late middle-age, the self-appointed cultural arbiters of the district; a veteran from the Vietnam War wanting to write a memoir; a long-haired young man who thinks that Jim Morrison of the Doors was the greatest poet who ever lived; and a sullen young girl who told me she has Nothing To Say because she has not Experienced Life. I read from the work-in-progress, which was fairly well received...

Elizabeth stopped writing because she felt the need to Experience Life. She put aside her pen and went downstairs. It wasn't busy, just a few people at tables and one bloke in orange and navy blue work clothes drinking at the bar. Elizabeth sat down next to him.

She decided to do some vox pop. 'What do you think about this, then?' she asked, indicating the paper.

He looked at the photo and shrugged. 'Their business...'

'I just don't know whether I should go or not. I knew the groom a long time ago. Do you have the Salvos here? I thought I'd try for a retro look and buy a nice Crimplene pantsuit.'

The young bogan looked at her with interest. 'You're a dyke?'

'Yeah, last time I looked.'

'My girlfriend has always wanted to sleep with another woman. We watch porn movies sometimes and she gets really turned on.' He took out his mobile. 'Whar'd'ya think?'

The girlfriend was a small-featured blonde, pretty in a bland, early Princess Diana kind of way.

Elizabeth tried to imagine any kind of erotic activity with her, failed, tried again. She shook her head. 'You'll have to try your luck somewhere else, mate.'

He put the phone away without comment. Elizabeth turned the pages to the sporting section and they spent some time discussing local cricket.

The following morning, she crossed the street to the park, where about fifty people were gathered. There were two police and, some distance away, two people holding placards about the wrath of God.

It was nice to be in the majority for a change. The 'bride' was somewhat younger than Marilyn, a fetching gel named Amber who I understand works as a teller in the NAB. She's quite attractive, with a pretty face spoilt by hair dyed a particularly outré shade of tangerine. Marilyn was suitably butch in a dark suit, the girlfriend wore a long white strapless frock. (Call me old-fashioned but I've never liked that as a look for bridal wear. It eschews all mystery.) Why do some gays deem it necessary to ape these outmoded rituals, based as they are on the patriarchal values of paternity and property rights? Don't get me wrong, we should have full civil rights and be able to get married, join the military and become clergy-people, do all the really stupid things hets do but one clings to one's romantic notions, doesn't one, that the world should really be one great big bisexual anarchist commune…

Here, Elizabeth paused to reflect on the irony of writing this sentence to Sarah who had never wanted anything from life except the standard middle-class rewards: house, reliable partner, interesting work, family.

Anyway, the happy couple kissed, to much applause. I caught Marilyn's eye, essayed a jolly wave and gave her the thumbs up. She took a few moments to remember me; then recognition dawned like a day in mid-July. But I was introduced to Amber, who had managed to team her hair with hot-pink nail polish and lippy. Marilyn's clearly happy. She got help for what her brother did then she went to AA for six years (still goes sometimes, apparently). She's a grandmother now. Her daughter Tania has two sons, she lives with the father who works at one of the timber mills. On the subject of kids, she remembered YOU. Marilyn did, I mean…

Elizabeth put down her pen. She was sitting in a coffee shop across from the pub, two days after the wedding. She flipped through the paper then put it aside and thought about Marilyn, who had been named for the iconic blonde actress. Marilyn's father had pissed off up north when she was a baby and her mother had lost interest in her soon after. Her brother had become very interested and that continued until Marilyn was sixteen, when she left home for good. Somewhere along the way, her daughter had been born, was taken away, given back, taken off her again.

Elizabeth pushed away her coffee cup and the plate which retained custardy vanilla slice crumbs. All this thinking about the past made her claustrophobic. She crossed the street, packed her things into the car and started towards the tree-covered hills. She left the bitumen and took a track which wound up and up then plunged down into a ravine and finally came to a stop beside a meandering creek. Beryl 2 galloped about, frisky as a three-year-old, the arthritis in her hind legs momentarily forgotten.

Elizabeth pitched her tent beneath some kind of deciduous European tree which should have stood in a suburban backyard but instead, by some trick of the wind, had ended up in a forest of eucalypts, a misfit with gracious boughs and verdant, over-lading leaves. Birds roosted in that tree and later in the night, Elizabeth woke to the hoarse screaming of a possum. She lay looking up at the stars through the tent opening, thinking back to that peculiar three-way meeting.

She and Marilyn had been lying on the bed, watching *The Bold and the Beautiful* when the doorbell rang. Elizabeth was too out of it to move, until a familiar face peered through the window, shading her eyes as she squinted into the darkness.

'Shit! Shit! It's my ex! What's she doing here? Shit!' Elizabeth slid off the bed and tried to tidy the piles of clothes on the floor but she was too drunk: if she moved around too much, she'd throw up. She collapsed back on the bed again, just as Sarah rang the doorbell.

'Come in, it's open.'

Sarah's pregnancy barely showed but she was dressed, ostentatiously Elizabeth thought, in expensive maternity clothes, a black velvet smock above flowing linen trousers. A matching black band held back her hair. She was doing that glowing thing that pregnant women are supposed to do.

'I'm looking for some notes I used to have,' she announced without preamble. 'I can't find them at home so I thought they must have accidentally ended up with you, when we cleared the St Kilda flat. I've come to collect them.'

'A phone call would have been nice.'

'I did phone. Three times. You must have a very busy social life at the moment, Lizzie. Your number's always engaged.'

Elizabeth shrugged. She and Marilyn often took the phone off the hook before they started. She looked at Sarah's slightly rounded stomach. 'Are you going to keep working until you drop the brat?'

'I'll be going on leave in a few months but before that I'm curating an exhibition about Australian women surrealists.'

'Well, you ought to be able to put that in one fairly small room.'

Marilyn, who had been watching Sarah with a mix of resentment, interest and incomprehension, now interjected eagerly, 'Oh, I've seen something about that. I seen it the other day on the telly.'

Sarah looked at her for a moment. 'And all that is seen and unseen passes away,' she remarked to no one in particular.

Elizabeth sniggered. She met Sarah's gaze and they laughed. How lovely it was to do this, to crush Marilyn's eggshell self-esteem and watch her shrink back. It was nasty, it was cruel, it was exhilarating. It made Elizabeth fall in love all over again. It made her see things she hadn't bothered noticing before: Marilyn's stained and faded windcheater, the gritty eyes and grimy mouth.

Sarah smoothed back her shining hair. 'Come on. Show me where I can find my stuff.'

Elizabeth, still carrying the Bundy bottle, led her into the room which passed as a study.

Sarah stood for a moment, looking around, before she turned on Elizabeth. 'Look at you! You're fat! You need a bath! I don't know what you think you're doing but you're not helping that woman and she obviously needs help! You're a...a co-dependent slob!'

At that, Elizabeth burst out laughing again. A trickle of the sticky liquor ran down her chin and she wiped it away with her sleeve. She glanced back at Marilyn to see whether she shared the joke but Marilyn had passed out, head lolling on the pillow, mouth slack.

Sarah strode silently through the doorway and picked up one of

Marilyn's small white hands. She pulled up the shirt sleeve to the elbow and turned the arm towards Elizabeth, who saw the looping red weals, a calligraphy of pain. Gently, Sarah replaced the hand on the bed.

She retraced her steps and started rummaging in a cupboard. 'Don't play with damaged people, Lizzie.'

'What makes you think I'm not one of those?'

'You're not damaged, you're just feeling sorry for yourself and it's gone on far too long.'

As Sarah scooped up a pile of notes, Elizabeth sneaked a look. It had nothing to do with Australian women surrealists, it was just some old academic verbiage, left over from Sarah's MA.

Sarah was checking up on her. Why? Was she worried? Perhaps it was something else; maybe the relationship with the tennis coach hadn't proved to be such a love match, after all.

Elizabeth raised the Bundy bottle and swigged. 'We've got off on the wrong foot, haven't we? How are you?'

'Me? I'm fine. Still a bit sick sometimes but apart from that, really good.'

'And Ange…?'

'Ange is great. Thrilled about the baby. Keeps going out and buying things.' Sarah laughed. 'There's all this stuff spilling out of the room we've set up as the nursery. You should see it!'

Elizabeth was glad she couldn't. She imagined night after sleepless night, cleaning up vomit and shit. She had seen her mother's enslavement and the rage which was the product of exhaustion, powerlessness and grief. No thanks. But Sarah knew all that: Elizabeth had told her, sitting on a beach at Mallacoota a couple of years ago.

Elizabeth watched the moon ascend through a membrane of copper-coloured cloud. She took the letter from her backpack

…and she asked how everything had gone with you. 'What happened to the pretty lady who came around to visit just before we broke up?' I told her you were disgracefully happy, everything had worked out, your kid was a credit to you, yada, yada, yada… Marilyn nodded sagely, as though that

was to be expected. 'She looked like someone who had good karma.' Good karma! Don't people believe in the most bizarre things?

Beryl 2, tethered beneath a tree, emitted a soft growl. The languid stipples of shadow cast by the moon wavered and shook as the wind momentarily freshened but there were no other sounds. 'You smell a fox, girl, smell a fox?'

Elizabeth decided she would leave out the rest of the conversation, the lies she had told Marilyn after the wedding: how well she was doing, the important job she had, the house she owned in Northcote. No, she could not put those in. She looked at her last sentence. Did Marilyn really believe that something she had done in a previous existence had been responsible for her brother's behaviour, this time round? When Elizabeth asked about him, Marilyn had pointed to the concrete monolith which was the town's water storage tower: 'He feels so guilty, he'd jump off, if I told him.' It must be amazing to have that much power over another human being. Perhaps, in the end, Marilyn had won.

Anyway, I've never thanked you for what you did for me back then, giving me that brisk verbal slapping and telling me to pull myself together. If it hadn't been for you, I might still be there, buried beneath a mountain of Jim Beam bottles (worse ways to go, I suppose.) Ah, the melodious silver music of the creek has had its affect. My eyelids droop, I flit, I float etc… Please convey my sincerest regards to Ange and tell my goddaughter I'll be in contact soon…

Next morning, Elizabeth washed in the creek, got right under and submerged herself. The water was so cold that for a moment her heart stopped; then that frail vessel resumed normal operation. She folded the tent away and harnessed Beryl to her customary position in the passenger seat. As she left the forest and turned the car onto the bitumen, a government vehicle, driven at speed, passed in the opposite direction. Elizabeth recognised her drinking partner from the pub, bound for work. She gave a matey wave and he responded with a cheerful, unrecognising grin.

There was a shop on the main street called Baubles, Buckles 'n' Beads, where Elizabeth purchased a fairly expensive red leather handbag; then she went to the local Target and bought a blender. The address Marilyn had given was in an area of public housing: the dwellings were not ugly or dilapidated but they had a neatness and utilitarianism which verged on the dreary. Elizabeth imagined daytime television and photographs of grandchildren on the walls. She sat with the engine idling for a couple of minutes then put the car into gear and drove away. It wouldn't hurt to have another blender. Her last stop before leaving was a red-brick building laced with wrought-iron Victorian curlicues. She went inside and bought a stamp.

How old-fashioned this was, posting a letter! Elizabeth weighed the envelope in her hand. But there it was: she and Sarah were from that far-off time before the internet and mobile phones; before the term 'gay marriage' became both commonplace and controversial. Sarah and Ange's daughter, Miriam Sophia, soon to begin first year uni, would look down her pierced nose, would call Elizabeth an environmental vandal and castigate her for using a product made from murdered trees. Elizabeth smiled. That was the sort of stuff kids said nowadays.

She flipped the letter through the slot in the box, feeling mildly transgressive. *I remember what you did for me back then…* It was the closest she would ever get to a love letter. The handbag would have to wait until she and Sarah caught up in person.

CPSIA information can be obtained
at www.ICGtesting.com
Printed in the USA
LVHW090317081119
636756LV00001B/4/P